D1648280

MARYSUE
RUCCI
BOOKS

ALSO BY JOHANNES LICHTMAN

Such Good Work

CALLING UKRAINE

JOHANNES LICHTMAN

MARYSUE
RUCCI
BOOKS

NEW YORK LONDON TORONTO SYDNEY NEW DELHI

An Imprint of Simon & Schuster, Inc.
1230 Avenue of the Americas
New York, NY 10020

This book is a work of fiction. Any references to historical events, real people, or real places are used fictitiously. Other names, characters, places, and events are products of the author's imagination, and any resemblance to actual events or places or persons, living or dead, is entirely coincidental.

First Marysue Rucci Books/Scribner hardcover edition April 2023

Interior design by Carly Loman

Manufactured in the United States of America

1 3 5 7 9 10 8 6 4 2

Library of Congress Cataloging-in-Publication Data has been applied for.

ISBN 978-1-9821-5681-7
ISBN 978-1-9821-5682-4 (ebook)

For Lance

CALLING UKRAINE

AUTHOR'S NOTE

In the early days of Russia's brutal invasion, a Ukrainian friend would send me videos of missiles hitting apartment buildings. I would toggle between rage, grief, and deep worry for all the friends and colleagues who had chosen to stay. But the day before Orthodox Easter, this friend sent a tutorial on cleaning your windows in preparation for the holiday. The video opens with a shot of a Ukrainian man holding up cleaning supplies. A breezy Earth, Wind, and Fire song plays in the background. Then the video cuts to the man's bombed-out window frame. End of tutorial.

As the war continued, my friend and I would try to Skype every few weeks. On August 24, we had arranged to Skype to celebrate Ukrainian Independence Day, but he had to cancel, since Russia was hammering Ukraine with rockets to ruin the holiday. When we were finally able to talk, he told me how, after several hours stuck in the bomb shelter with the air raid sirens blaring, the man next to him said, "What are they doing—bringing that rocket in on a bicycle?"

"The Ukrainian sense of humor originated from all the troubles that preceded our people for centuries," my friend said. The choice, he explained, was to give up and cry, or fight and laugh at the enemy. "We chose the latter!"

I wrote *Calling Ukraine* before Russia launched its full-scale invasion. The story takes place in 2018–19, during the period between the Maidan Revolution and the Russian invasion—a time of great hope from the changes happening in Ukraine, coupled with resignation at the things that would likely never change. Also: a time of political upheaval, as a popular actor announced his candidacy for president.

But after February 24, 2022, I felt compelled to change the novel. The humor now felt inappropriate. Any ambivalence the characters felt toward the presidential candidate, Zelensky, now read, to me, like Kremlin propaganda. When I'd written the novel, most Americans couldn't name the president of Ukraine. Now Zelensky was an international symbol of heroism—why point out the criticisms that had preceded his election?

The problem was that the more I tried to rewrite the book, the less true it felt. Humor was a defining feature of the time I spent in Ukraine. And the fact that many were skeptical of Zelensky does not lessen his accomplishments. As another friend wrote to me from Lutsk, "A year ago, none of us Ukrainians could have thought we would be so proud of our president." Ukraine has a heroic president who is also a comedian; that must say something about the country.

In the end, I left the novel almost completely intact. (Though I did take out a few mini-rants about Russian disinformation's influence on Western media in the post-Maidan period, since that disinformation had now been effectively countered.) But I left in the jokes, and I left in the Zelensky skepticism. I hope that this was the right decision. Even if it wasn't, I take comfort in knowing that most Americans are already well aware of the bravery and suffering of Ukrainians and don't need a novel to explain it to them. My hope, now that everything has changed, is that this book may, if nothing else, give a tiny glimpse at what life in Ukraine looked like before the invasion, and why it's so worth fighting for.

Johannes Lichtman
November 21, 2022
Washington, DC

SEPTEMBER 2018

Davey had a proposal. We'd met in college and though we had almost nothing in common, he liked me and thought I was smarter than I was, which it turned out was enough to sustain over a decade of friendship. Since graduation, he'd email me once or twice a year to tell me, for example, about a dream he had that he wanted to turn into a screenplay—did I want to write it for him?—or to pitch a start-up that allowed members to rent books for a low monthly fee. This time, he wanted to know if I'd be interested in heading up support ops at the Ukrainian office of his short-term rental start-up. Apparently, he'd come across an article I wrote a few years earlier on the booming Airbnb scene in Tbilisi, which was enough to make him believe that I was an expert on short-term rentals and former Soviet republics.

His message arrived on a rainy Monday, which was my Saturday, and I found myself reluctant to get out of bed, dreading the two empty days ahead of me, despite having looked forward to them all week. I was lying on a knock-off bed frame from China that looked almost identical to the more expensive American version, which I'd ordered a few months earlier, when Maureen and I broke up, but which had only just arrived. After so many notifications about back orders and delays, my anticipation had built to the point where the bed frame's arrival had come to symbolize the end of my old life and the beginning of something new and exciting. But then I assembled it, slept on it, woke up, and remembered that it was just a bed frame.

When I looked up Davey's new venture, I found that it wasn't just a half-baked idea with a sleekly designed website, but instead a real company doing real business, featured in articles in real-sounding publications.

"In less than a year, we've become the sixth-largest short-term-rental provider in the US," Davey told me over the phone later that day, quoting himself from the articles. He said they were already making huge inroads in New York, San Francisco, and other cities that had been hostile to Airbnb, by working with private apartment buildings that already had hotel licenses. These buildings partnered with Davey's company instead of Airbnb because they were self-policing, Davey explained. They ran background checks and set up noise monitors in their apartments, and if the noise passed a certain level the tenant would get a text warning. If they didn't comply, they were evicted.

"Good neighbors," he said as I read along with the slogan bannered across the top of the site, "make the world a better place."

A major part of their philosophy, he told me, was innovative technology, fearlessly implemented—which meant smart-sourcing software developers.

"The average Ukrainian salary is three hundred dollars a month. Which means that if I offer developers there twenty-five hundred dollars per month, it's a *crazy* amount of money. We can hire absolutely top-end, cream-of-the-crop Ukrainian developers to do the coding for what I'd pay a cashier at a Seattle McDonald's. The Ukrainian developers are almost as good as the American ones, they cost a fraction of the price, and they never, ever demand a better kombucha station."

I pointed out that I didn't know anything about coding. When people mentioned "coding" I flashed to lines of green text sprawling across a black background of a nineties computer screen, an image I was pretty sure came from the movie *Hackers*.

"Patience, Turner." Davey laughed like this was an old joke between us. "I'm getting to that."

He said that the next step was optimizing the Ukrainian software developers' offices to double as call centers. That's where I came in. They were in the early stages of the first such project: a small center with five agents, run out of the already-established developers' office in Lutsk, an "up-and-coming city" near the Polish border in western Ukraine. The problem, he said, was that, while the Ukrainian call center agents meticulously followed instructions, they were struggling to acclimate to American conversational styles. In particular: small talk, friendliness, and not scaring the shit out of customers.

"They sound less like they want to help you with your booking and more like they want to harvest your data to find and then kill you."

He said they'd hired a local English professor, a Ukrainian, to supervise, but that she was just teaching them grammar instead of anything useful.

"When they're not scaring the customers, they're too quiet. They just type and wait for the pages to load. We told them to fill the gap with light conversation, so they started saying, 'How old are you? You have children? Why not?' We need an American to show them how to sound natural. And to knock the classroom British out of them. Get them to stop saying 'fortnight,' 'flat,' 'lorry,' and whatever."

"Why are they talking about lorries?"

"I don't know, man." There was a pause, and the silence had the distinct shape of Davey reading another message. "Customer service is improvisation. That's why I need someone like you."

"*X* is improvisation" was a statement that could be made about pretty much anything, but I was still a little flattered. "What exactly is it that you want me to do?"

"I want you to take the five-thousand-dollar relocation bonus I'm going to send you as soon as we get off the phone and buy a plane ticket. I want you to send me an invoice for whatever it costs to break your lease. I want you to move to Ukraine in two weeks. I want you to live there for the next year—at least. I want you to teach the agents how to provide the level of customer support that Americans are accustomed to. After you've shown them how to master that on the phone, I want you to teach them to do it on email, SMS, and chat support so they can handle all our tickets. We're currently getting about seventy thousand tickets a year, and that's only going to go up. We need them to be more efficient. More natural. More conversational." He laughed. "And I want you to have the fucking time of your life in Ukraine."

The problem with people like Davey was that they would rather hire someone they know, who might be qualified, than find someone they didn't know, who was certifiably qualified. The problem with people like me was that I didn't have a good reason to say no to people like Davey.

"The pay is thirty-six thousand dollars a year, which I know isn't much in the US—but in Ukraine? You can live like a king. You can rent a nice apartment with a maid, a cook, and even a live-in hooker."

I ignored the part about pressing the locals into servitude as a perk of the job and repeated the salary offer out loud a few times as if I was thinking about it. Then I started thinking about it. When a shift manager position had opened up at my restaurant, I'd turned it down—manager was a vocation, whereas I was just working there to support my journalism. But after nearly eight years of freelance magazine writing, I was thirty years old and hardly any closer to breaking through. And my apartment was so ugly.

I had imagined this apartment, a studio in Southeast Portland, as a place of freedom. After my dad died, I started feeling so lonely with Maureen that I decided that it would be better to just be alone, since at least then the loneliness would make sense. I had imagined that being single—relieved of the burden of another person's presence, attention, and disappointment—would make me freer to feel whatever I was feeling, and that what I was feeling would, eventually, be happiness. The first month or two of singledom had been exciting—there were dating apps now, and on these apps were women who wanted to meet me!—but soon the anxiety of dating overtook the excitement. No matter how these dates went, they would leave me feeling guilty and lonely. If there was no chemistry, I would feel like I'd let my date down, and if we ended up sleeping together, I would feel as if I'd tricked her into it, even if she was the one who'd initiated the sex. If she wanted to meet again and I didn't, I would feel guilty for hurting her, and if I wanted to meet again, but she didn't respond, I would feel very lonely. I wasn't happier than I'd been with Maureen—but neither was I sadder, which made me think I'd made the right decision.

And now I found myself surrounded by these custard-colored walls, which were just as bare as the day I signed the lease, struggling to think of a single thing keeping me in Portland.

"Okay," I said to Davey. "I'm in."

I LANDED IN KYIV, BUT MY SUITCASES DIDN'T, SO I SPENT FOUR days exploring the capital and waiting for my bags. On the first day, I established that it was a terrifying city that made no sense. There was less smiling and fewer English speakers than anywhere I'd visited. The boulevards were oceanic, built as if some optimistic dictator was planning for the day when everyone had a car. I couldn't find anywhere to cross the street until I realized that the crosswalks were underground—that what I'd thought were stairs to the metro actually led across the street. The calm chaos of the traffic suggested everyone was expertly marching to a beat I couldn't hear, and I kept bracing for a crash that never came. The golden onion church domes had something sinister in their glow. The brutalist housing blocs looked like collective punishment. Even the four- and five-story Old World apartment buildings—the pretty kind that you'd see in any European capital, with their light colors, hundred-year-old bones, and little balconies hanging off the edge, cramped with iron patio furniture facing the sun—looked like they'd just been in a fight. But I calmed myself with the knowledge that this could all be material. Even though I wasn't a journalist anymore, I wasn't ready to stop seeing the world as if I was going to write about it.

So when I struggled to find food that first day, it wasn't just a frustrating morning—it was a story. The absence of English speakers was an impediment, as were the handwritten chalkboard menus, since handwritten Cyrillic was a different species from the typed characters I'd studied before leaving Portland. After much searching, I eventually bought what I thought was a croissant from a street vendor. It was not a croissant but a cold hot dog wrapped in puff pastry, which, despite my hunger, was inedible. I threw it away, looked out at the Dnipro River—which, like all urban rivers, resembled a big dirty bathtub draining to nowhere—and almost buckled under a wave of jet lag that made it feel like I didn't live on this planet. I eventually found what looked like a hamburger chain with a digital menu on the wall.

In the afternoon, feeling a little better after my food, I walked through a lush park in central Kyiv with deeply dipping hills, tall trees, and packs of teenagers drinking and laughing and posing for pictures around every corner. Each couple strolling through the park that day consisted of a very good-looking woman—often holding flowers or a teddy bear or some other gendered gift—with a not-so-good-looking man. Before coming to Ukraine, I'd tried to do my research to prepare me, but there was a limited amount of English-language information available for the prospective traveler. I'd found, uncomfortably, that the best sources of basic information about where you could use credit cards, which banks had reliable ATMs, and how Ukrainian rental contracts worked were not tourism sites, travel blogs, or Ukraine guides, but message boards maintained by American, British, and Canadian men sharing notes on how to sleep with and/or marry Ukrainian women.

When I went to the message boards to check if I could pay by card on the Kyiv metro, I learned: *The Kyiv metro is an old-fashioned system that uses tokens. You'll have to pay cash to buy tokens, so bring exact change if you don't want to be scolded by the lady at the window. The fare is cheap (roughly 20 cents), the trains run on time, the system is relatively safe, and the metro can take you to all the best districts for nightclubs and cafés (see my post in "Kyiv Nightlife"). But be aware that a lot of Ukrainian women are criminals who will charge you for an "interpreter" during your date, and even the ones who aren't criminals are cock teases.*

The men on the message boards believed that Ukraine was a great country for foreigners to meet a nice girl with "traditional values," which was shorthand for an attractive woman who will gratefully sleep with and/or marry an unattractive man. What bothered me about the men wasn't just their sexism—the internet, and world for that matter, was full of sexists I rarely gave much thought to. It bothered me that this was the image Ukrainians would have when they thought of an American man: the entitled and aggressive losers who'd been arriving since the fall of the Soviet Union under the belief that they deserved to have sex with women far better looking than they were.

When I'd gone through passport control at Boryspil, the officer behind the glass had asked me where I was going in Ukraine. When I answered, "Lutsk," she'd looked up from my passport.

"Girl?" she'd said, in the same tone you might say, *Business or pleasure?*

I'd spent the rest of my time at the airport trying hard to avoid even glancing at any women. But walking through the park that day in Kyiv, I couldn't help but notice the gender inequality at play in real-life Ukrainian couples. Maybe a scarcity of supply meant that okay-looking guys here could date supermodels. Maybe a century of oppression, conscription, and mass murder—first by the Soviets, then by the Nazis, then by the Soviets again, and then, after the fall of the Soviet Union, by gangster-businessmen who had seized most of the country's wealth in the nineties—had depleted the Ukrainian male population. Or maybe it was just an anomaly. I couldn't assume that a dozen couples in a Kyiv park on a sunny day represented all of Ukraine. By that measure, the Ukrainians who saw me walking around in my luggage-less state would think all American men wore Adidas sweatpants with running shoes and Levi's jeans jackets—and didn't shave.

But after a few days in Kyiv, I decided that the park had not been an aberration and that this was a country with a disparity in physical attractiveness between the genders. It occurred to me that someone like me—a tall and rich, at least by Ukrainian standards, foreigner, who, once his clothes arrived, would be well-dressed—might do well with women here. I indulged the fantasy of dipping my toe into a dating pool of Ukrainian women with sharp cheekbones and expectations set low enough that I might be a catch. But if the anxiety of dating in America was bad, it would be much worse in a country where I didn't speak the language or understand the customs. If the guilt of transactional sex was bad in America, I imagined it would be terrible in a country that Americans had been exploiting for decades. Besides, I was not here to meet women.

I had made the decision before leaving Portland that I would take a year off dating. Being abstinent at home would have felt kind of pathetic, but doing it abroad made it more like a journey of personal discovery—something you might pitch as a longform article or even a book one day. It made me feel good, too, to know that while most American men were coming here for sex, I was doing the opposite.

By my last day in Kyiv, I started to see how the city could've actually been the beautiful metropolis I'd read about online had I been a different person there under different circumstances. The constellations of golden domes shining in the sunlight. The metro stations with their barrel-vaulted ceilings and real-life chandeliers dangling overhead. The Dnipro River, which at night transformed from a big dirty bathtub to a sheet of glass sparkling with city lights. But even so, Kyiv was only a layover, and by the time my luggage finally arrived I was ready to go.

When the driver I'd hired pulled into Lutsk, a city of about two hundred thousand six hours west of the capital where I was to live for the next year, I felt immediately at home. I was calmed by the normal width of the boulevards and crosswalks luxuriously placed almost every block. Nobody smiled or spoke English here either, but they seemed less personally angry at me than the pedestrians in Kyiv had. The architecture wasn't exactly pretty, but neither was it intimidating: two-story storefronts with rounded facades that looked a little bit like false fronts and blocky functionalist concrete that made me think of bell-bottoms. Little yellow buses scuttled in and out of traffic in the city center, and people drank tea and coffee at sidewalk cafés late into the evening. Had I landed first in Lutsk, I would've probably had the same reaction as when I landed in Kyiv: *This is the most different place that I've ever been.* But after Kyiv, the little town felt safe.

The next day, I walked fifteen minutes from my apartment to Davey's call center, which was housed on the second floor of a boxy new building by the river. I knocked on the door and a handsome man in his mid-twenties opened. He was dressed in designer jeans and a black T-shirt, with dark hair cropped close on the sides and a little longer on top. He wore a look on his face that just a few days earlier I would have thought was disdain but now recognized as the resting neutral expression of Ukrainians.

"Hi, I'm Turner. I'm here to head up support ops."

"Yes, we are expecting you. Nice to meet you." The man shook my hand, introduced himself as Dima, and said he was a senior associate software developer. "But tell me please, Turner, don't Americans go by their first names? Or by 'Mister' and then the family name?"

"Yes. You're correct, Dima. But—" But what? I was a thirty-year-old manager. Why was I introducing myself by my last name? "I was under the impression that Ukrainians had difficulty pronouncing 'John.' I thought 'Turner' would be easier."

"Yes, you're correct, John." Dima's "John" was somewhere between "gin" and "June." "But if you only say the words we know, maybe we won't learn so much?" Dima laughed, and I joined in. At first it was a polite laugh, but soon I felt my face breaking into a real smile. It was the first time someone had laughed with me in Ukraine.

Dima showed me around the office, which looked like the set from a movie about the 2000s American tech boom: beanbag chairs, a gaming console, and desk pods filled an open single room, built under the idea that employees wouldn't hate their coworkers enough to need walls or doors. At the center of the room were eight software developers' desks with big monitors, but my domain was the five call center desks near the door. The agents were just settling in for their 4:00 p.m.–to–midnight shift. Two of the agents were boys who couldn't have been more than twenty-one, and two were women in their late twenties to early thirties. One of the desks was empty, but no sooner had I noticed its vacancy than the door opened and a woman walked in. She was about my age, with long brown hair that crested over her forehead in a wave. She was fair, slim without being bony, and her washed-out jeans with white sneakers and a beige corduroy jacket struck me as the perfect outfit for the day. I had worked for many managers but had never been a manager myself, and I was determined to be a good, bland boss, who made my employees' jobs easier without having any effect on their personal lives. So it was with dismay that I found myself so immediately attracted to her.

I introduced myself to all the agents, and when I got to her and she said her name was Natalie I tried to banish the thought that we had known each other in a previous life—which, despite my not believing in past lives, was a thought that often hit me when I saw a woman to whom I was very attracted.

"It's nice to meet you," I said when I shook her hand, feeling the surprising length of her fingers, then immediately releasing them.

"But how could you possibly know?" Natalie said, in a not-so-harsh but definitely still noticeable accent.

"How could I know what?"

"That it's nice to meet me."

"It's an American expression!" said a woman I assumed was Oksana, the English teacher, who had appeared from nowhere and was now in front of me, wearing bright red lipstick, a knee-length red skirt, black leather boots, a black top, and a red blazer. Her hair was blond, her fingernails were painted red, and while I couldn't tell if she was in her thirties, forties, or fifties, she had the vibe of someone who would never die. "You know this."

Natalie shrugged at Oksana in a way that could have meant anything.

I shook Oksana's hand and told her that it was nice to meet her, too.

"Frankly speaking," she said, "it is my pleasure," while wordlessly conveying that it was very much not. I assumed that my hiring was a demotion for her, which meant that there was no reason for her to like me. But there was something in me that believed that everyone should like me, and it unnerved me that she didn't.

When I turned to address the room, I found my mouth was dry. My shirt—a designer white button-up recently returned from the airline, which just an hour earlier had fit perfectly—was now too tight in the shoulders, bunched up at the waist, and sticking to my armpits from the sweat. I hadn't expected to be nervous. I was teaching them how to speak English like an American, one of the few topics on which I could be called an expert.

"Good afternoon, everyone. My name is John Turner, and I'm really looking forward to working with you." I apologized for being late—explained why I'd been stranded in Kyiv—then regretted the apology, as it probably made me look weak. I felt the dryness spreading across my tongue and looked up at the clock on the wall, which read 3:54. "We only have a few minutes before the lines open, but let's do a little warm-up. How is everyone doing today?"

There was silence. Which I'd expected from Davey's warning.

"Kyle," I said to a boy with a blond crewcut who looked like he was years away from growing facial hair. "How are you doing today?"

"So far, so good," said Kyle, monotone. His accent was apparent, but his words didn't come from as far back in his throat as most Ukrainians I'd met, making his English sound a little less, though still very, bassy.

"Very good. And what's your real name, Kyle?"

"Kyle."

"Great," I said. I didn't know whether it was more insulting to call the agents by their American names or insist that they give their Ukrainian names, but I decided to push this question back to another day. "And what would you ask me, Kyle, if I were a customer and we were going to make small talk?"

"How is your day going, sir?"

"It's going pretty well. I'm loving this weather we're having."

There was silence for a while.

"My father doesn't like the heat," said Andy, who had a small bun knotted tightly behind gelled-back hair and wore a green T-shirt that said *Sacramento Clothing Company* in deliberately faded letters. "But he has been very morose since my mother became ill."

I paused. "This is what we call a good teaching moment. Andy, I'm very sorry to hear about your mother. And 'morose' is a high-level word in English. So well done there. But your mother's illness is not something you want to talk to the customers about. It might make them uncomfortable."

"When they ask how you're doing," Oksana said, "they don't really want to know how you are doing. They are lying."

"While Oksana is correct, sort of," I said, "I wouldn't say they're *lying*. It's just that they want a very limited answer to the question. It's not a lie so much as a euphemism. Does anyone know what a euphemism is?"

"It's when you use one word or phrase to disguise another word or phrase that might be unpleasing to the listener," Oksana said. "Like 'water closet' for 'toilet.'"

"Yes, that's correct, Oksana, but I was hoping that the agents could answer—"

"But, tell me please, how is 'How are you doing?' a euphemism? What unpleasing word or phrase are you attempting to disguise?"

The heat ran into my face with the realization that it was not a euphemism. I should have prepared better. Davey had said that the Ukrainians were so quiet. But Oksana was not quiet. I panicked and tried to remember what a preposition was, just in case she brought up prepositions.

"Very good point, Oksana. In this example, they're trying to disguise the fact that, as you said, they don't care how you're doing. They're checking the box of being polite while—"

"Tell me please, what do you mean by 'checking the box'?" Oksana said.

My objectives, as Davey had laid them out, were to guide the agents through the art of small talk, improve their ability to sound natural and conversational, and reduce the average call time from twelve to eight minutes so that the agents could start taking on email and chat tickets as well. It was only now that I was realizing that I had no idea how I was supposed to accomplish any of this. Luckily, we were out of time.

"That's a great question! But it's almost four o'clock, which means it's almost nine a.m. in New York—we'll have to put a pin in this," I said, rushing forward as I realized I'd used another euphemism. "But I'm really looking forward to picking it up tomorrow!"

I retreated to my desk, marked by an A4 sheet of printer paper in a translucent binder page with my name written in blue Comic Sans font, by the back wall of the office. Davey had somehow convinced me that I would be useful here just by virtue of my presence, and I felt very stupid for having believed him. I took out my laptop and spent the rest of the shift doing what I should have been doing since I accepted the job offer: researching how to run quality control for customer support.

Once I realized how unprepared for the job I was, I spent days researching and outlining a comprehensive plan of attack. Step one, as I wrote to Davey, was to start recording all our calls. Step two was to analyze the ones with the longest call times and the ones with repeat callers. Davey probably didn't read the next eighteen steps of my plan before writing back that he loved the enthusiasm. But he reminded me that this wasn't Apple—it was a call center with five agents. He suggested I just grab some headphones and start listening in.

Once I did so, it didn't take too many calls to notice that a major problem was, in fact, a struggle to improvise and still sound American. The agents seemed to revert to an un-American directness whenever they had to go off script.

"No, we cannot do this," Andy would say to a customer, without an "unfortunately" at the beginning. And then Oksana would be right over Andy's shoulder, whisper-yelling his mistake before I could even consider how to turn the mistake into a teaching moment.

This directness, I'd come to notice, wasn't rude in Ukrainian. My Ukrainian was still very limited, but I'd noticed that in a Ukrainian restaurant you wouldn't say, *Could I get the bill?* You would say, *Bring me the bill.* I wasn't sure how to convince the agents that the thing they'd always thought was polite—saying directly and imperatively what they meant—was actually very rude.

The bigger challenge than directness—which, though counter-intuitive, was at least concrete—was small talk. Or, more generally, building rapport. Rapport building could be accomplished without small talk, through things like active listening and showing care on a person-to-person level. But we had a system that was prone to lag. Whenever an agent had to look something up, there was a long lull. The agents could ask the table-setting questions from the script, but once they had to improvise, it wasn't just a question of forgetting the right way to do it, but of not understanding how to do it in the first place.

When I listened in with Angie—who was probably thirty or so and wore sequins stitched to her jeans and T-shirts with pink text that spelled out things like "rock and roll girl"—I found that she knew how to ask a customer about the weather in Fort Worth this time of year. But when the customer said that it broke a hundred again yesterday, she would answer, "Okay." In Ukrainian, "okay" was apparently a versatile word that could mean, "good," "yes," "I understand," "okay," or "okay!" But in English, "okay" meant: "This is the conclusion of this line of conversation." Just like she was wearing American clothes in a way that probably made sense in a Ukrainian context but was confusing in an American one, she was also speaking English from a Ukrainian perspective. But I couldn't explain that any more than I could explain that her jeans were designed for a twelve-year-old.

I learned that asking, "How are you doing today?" made the agents particularly uncomfortable. Apparently, in Ukraine, you would never ask a customer how they were doing. This was an incredibly personal and not-at-all casual question, reserved for friends and family. Which wasn't to say that Ukrainians didn't talk about trivial things—I assumed they did—but they didn't seem to do it in the same way as Americans, and they didn't do it with strangers.

I came up with simple examples and exercises, but no matter how well they appeared to go over, they proved to have no application beyond the specific situations we practiced. After two weeks of trying to pool common mistakes into learning exercises, I instead decided to try sitting in on the best agents to see what they were doing right.

"So far, so good, cannot complain, thank you for asking," Kyle told a customer while I listened in. "And how is your day going? . . . Very good. Let me check that for you. The unit is currently occupied, and the tenants will check out by eleven. Which means we will have the unit cleaned then and try to get it ready for you as soon as possible. . . . No. We cannot guarantee that it will be ready early. But if it is ready before your four o'clock check-in, I will contact you personally to let you know."

His English was still clipped and formal, but he didn't seem uncomfortable transitioning between small talk and business, and he clearly yet politely expressed the pertinent information. I made notes on everything he was doing right. He said "very good" instead of "okay" in response to the customer's response. He had said "no" when the customer asked if they should plan on the place being ready early, which wasn't great, but followed it up with, "We cannot guarantee," and said he would contact them if the situation changed. After the call, I took out my earbud and asked Kyle how he'd gotten so comfortable in the language. He said that he was used to speaking English from playing video games. I knew that Andy also played video games and he was easily the worst agent, so video game experience alone did not make an effective agent. But I didn't know what question to ask to learn how Kyle brought his video game experience to the phones.

It was clear, fairly early on, that the best agent—not necessarily at sounding American, but at being present and empathetic—was

Natalie. At first, I'd questioned this assessment, wondering if it was just my attraction to her that was making her every word sound smarter. But I noticed that the other agents would transfer their most difficult customers over to Natalie. I'd tried to stay away from her desk, not wanting to get too close for fear of being a bad boss. But it occurred to me that ignoring her because I was attracted to her was almost as bad as paying attention to her because I was attracted to her. This evening, I pulled up a chair, put on a professional face, plugged in my earbuds, and listened in to see what she could teach the other agents.

"Yes, hello, Mr. Stevens," Natalie said. "I am aware of the email you are referencing. I am very sorry to deliver unpleasant news, but I'm afraid that the owner of the unit has sold the property, so we can no longer rent it to you."

She paused.

"Yes, exactly. We cannot rent it because we no longer have a contract with the owner."

She listened.

"You are absolutely right to be angry. We are very angry as well. It came as a total shock to us. We did not expect him to sell without any warning, and, frankly speaking, we were quite disappointed that a partner would show such disregard for our customers."

A pause.

"Yes, I am so sorry. And I can absolutely understand that—it has been very stressful for us as well."

It has been stressful for us as well. She was good.

"I have found three options for you that are similar size and location," Natalie said. "But I must warn you that the price difference is step."

"Steep!" Oksana hissed through clenched teeth, appearing quickly enough to startle me. "Not step, steep!"

"Please excuse me, Mr. Stevens, the price difference is quite *steep*. I will tell you about these other options."

There were little things to work on, sure—the last sentence should have been a question: *Can I tell you about these options now and we can see if any of them are a good fit?*—but there were so many little things she did to show the customer that she was on his team. I was furiously scribbling notes in my book when I was stopped by the sound of Kyle's voice across the room getting louder, much louder than normal. Not yelling, exactly, but growing shaky, like it might break at any second.

"Yes, of course, sir, my name is Kyle. *K-y-l-e.* My last name? Kravchenko. *K-r-a*— No? Okay, yes, that is all right. Unfortunately, I cannot connect you with a supervisor in this office, as we do not have a supervisor present, but if you'd be willing to hold, I can connect you to our senior agent, who is on a call at the moment. Or I can give you a number to call for another office where a supervisor will be present. Would you like— . . . Yes, I understand, and I'm very sorry that I cannot refund your reservation, but per the user agreement— . . . Yes. Yes, I understand, sir, but this is not possible, because— Yes. . . . Yes. . . . Yes. Again, this is not possible. The terms of the reservation— . . . No. I cannot do that. No. Sir, unfortunately— . . . Sir, you agreed to the terms of— . . . But sir, I didn't do that. I do not have any control— . . . Hello? Sir? Sir, are you still on the line? Hello?" Kyle tapped a button on his keyboard, took a deep breath, and then threw down his headset. "You fucking little bitch!"

No one said anything. But I saw that all the agents had a hand over their mics as if there was a procedure in place for when this happened.

I walked over to Kyle's desk, leaned down, and asked him to join me in the hall.

"Everything okay?" I asked, after closing the door.

"Yes."

"I've never seen you get upset like that before. What did the customer say?"

"He . . ." Kyle paused. "He was very rude."

"I understand. But a lot of customers are rude."

Kyle shrugged.

"Was there something he said that was particularly rude?"

He was quiet for a minute. "He thought that I was an idiot."

I sighed and nodded. Maureen had complained that when she told me about someone who'd upset her I would get all quiet and withdrawn, like I didn't care or thought she was being crazy. But that wasn't it at all. I just got so mad that I wasn't in the room anymore. I was off kicking the shit out of the person who'd wronged her. I wanted to kick the shit out of the customer who'd insulted Kyle. But it wasn't my job to save Kyle. It was my job to be a good, calm boss, who showed empathy but also set clear boundaries.

"He's wrong, Kyle. You're very smart. I'd like to see him conduct a transaction in Ukrainian. I'm sorry you had to deal with such a disrespectful person." I looked for signs that I'd consoled Kyle, but his face was unreadable. "That said, you still can't react like that. When you yell, even if you wait until after the call is over, it bleeds through to every other call. It's unprofessional. Unacceptable."

"Yes."

"Dealing with disrespectful people is part of the job. That's part of why it pays so well."

I thought back to working at the restaurant, where rich twenty-somethings would call you over in the middle of a rush to say, "I'm so sorry, but—" and then make a totally unreasonable request or petty complaint. The thing that pissed me off wasn't their obliviousness to the demands facing the staff at this understaffed restaurant, but their belief that apologizing in the first half of the sentence ensured that nothing said in the second half could make them sound like a bad person. They could so easily insulate their self-regard from their behavior. I preferred the boomer dads who came in with their adult children and showed complete awareness of what assholes they were being. To keep from losing it, at the end of every "I'm so sorry, but . . ." complaint, I would imagine that the person was giving me a hug, consoling me for my father's death. It was a weird coping mechanism, but it sometimes worked.

"I find that it helps to have a strategy to deal with rudeness," I told Kyle. "That way, you already have the tools in place that you can use in situations when your anger is going to make it hard to think."

"I have a strategy," Kyle said. "I imagine I'm wearing a bulletproof vest. The vest is Kyle. Nothing they say can hurt me. It's all going into my vest. It's all going into Kyle."

"That's a good strategy. Make yourself bulletproof." I paused. "But what happened to the vest today?"

"Frankly speaking, I don't know. Maybe he shot me in the arm."

"Fair enough," I said. "But could you make sure it doesn't happen again?"

"Okay."

After Kyle left, I took a moment to regain my composure. My mouth was suddenly very dry. I went back inside for a drink of water but found that I'd forgotten to fill my bottle before leaving the house. I took the empty bottle from my backpack and started to fill it from the sink.

"What are you doing?" said a voice. It was Natalie, suddenly right next to me, turning off the tap. She was wearing a black turtleneck and her eyebrows looked perfect. She smelled like a perfume that girls wore when I was fifteen, and, for a second, I was alone with a girl in the dark of a movie theater for the first time, hands cold with sweat, wondering what I was supposed to do. "You can't drink the water from the pipes," Natalie said. "Have you been drinking this water?"

I had not been drinking the water. Ukraine, I knew from studying message boards before arriving, had the worst water in Europe. Even Ukrainians didn't drink the tap water.

"No." I shook my head in embarrassment. "I just forgot where I was for a second. Is there somewhere around here that you can get bottled water?"

Natalie led me up a flight of stairs to the top floor, where we walked through an office filled with Ukrainians on computers, then into a kitchen. On the counter was a digital espresso machine and a giant jug of water with a plastic pump attached to the top. She handed me a little paper cup.

"This is going to be a stupid question," I said.

"There is no such thing as a stupid question," Natalie said.

"Is that an expression here, too?"

"No. But when Davey came to visit, he gave a motivational seminar, and every time someone asked a stupid question, he said there was no such thing as a stupid question. I've been waiting to use it ever since."

"And this is the first chance you've had?"

"Yes. To be honest, the customers rarely say, 'This is going be a stupid question.' But please, John, tell me your stupid question."

"How do I get the water out?"

"You're right. That's a very stupid question."

I laughed. Natalie took the cup, held it under the flimsy plastic spout, and pumped the large button on top. After two or three pumps, water began to flow.

"You don't have this in your home?" she said.

"I didn't even know these existed."

"How do you get your water?"

"I've been buying jugs from the mini-market."

"And then you carry it upstairs yourself?"

"Yes."

"And then you lift the whole jug up to pour into a glass every time you need to drink?" She mimed lifting a giant object, which wasn't that far off.

"Yes."

She laughed. "John, you can have your water delivered. Everyone does. My husband is a water delivery man."

My stomach sank a little. I looked at Natalie's bare left ring finger. But her ring was on the right hand. For a second, I flashed to an image of her in my bed, the hunger of her kiss, the heat of an affair. But I scrubbed it from my brain. Besides the fact that she was my employee, I wasn't going to pursue an affair, because I wasn't a shitty person. I certainly wasn't going to try to have the first affair of my life here in Ukraine like just another sexpat looking to get laid.

I drained the water to cover any thoughts my face might be betraying. "I should give him a call!" I said cheerfully. Maybe this was a blessing. With her being married, it might not be inappropriate for me to be friends with her, if she wanted. And I liked the idea of friendship without the pressure of more. But something about my joking that I should hire her husband seemed to have made her uncomfortable, and she quickly changed the subject.

"You have children?" Natalie said.

"No."

"Why not?"

"I think a woman needs to be involved for that to happen."

"This is a joke?"

"A very good one."

"Okay." She shrugged. "You're not married?"

"No."

"But you like women."

"I do."

"So why are you not married?"

"I'm not sure. I was together with a woman for four years. But it didn't work out."

Natalie didn't say anything. I held my cup under the pump and pushed the button—which offered the same resistance as a bike pump—until the water started to flow.

"Do you have children?" I said.

"No."

"Why not?"

She shrugged. "There's plenty of time."

"And you're married, I understand."

"Yes."

Like most of the conversations I'd had in Ukraine, either there were no rules or I didn't know the rules. The downside was constant anxiety, but the upside was being able to say pretty much whatever popped into your head. "Why?"

"Why what?"

"Why did you marry your husband?"

"Because I was in love with him."

I noted the past tense—wondered if it was intentional. "That's a good reason."

"Tell me, John, is this an example of good small talk?"

"No. This is terrible small talk."

"That was a joke."

"Oh! A very good one, too."

"But may I ask you a serious question?"

"Why stop now?"

"I have asked Oksana this as well, but I don't think she knows the answer. And I asked Davey when he visited, and he said that it was a good question, but then he didn't answer the question."

"That sounds like him. But please—there's no such thing as a stupid question."

"Okay. I understand that we are supposed to small-talk with the customers. I understand that I cannot ask them if they have children, or if they are married, or any question that could have an interesting answer. The weather, where they're calling from, if they are traveling for business or pleasure—I understand that these are the subjects we are supposed to talk about. What I don't understand is why."

"Why you need to small-talk?"

"Yes. Why not just be quiet if you don't have anything to say?"

I finished my water. "That is a good question, Natalie."

"Yes. But I already knew that."

"Right." I smiled and tried to hide the fact that I didn't have the answer. "If I'm being totally honest, it hadn't occurred to me that it was something I should explain. But now that you mention it, I can see that it's important. Important enough that I think the rest of the team should hear the answer as well. Do you mind if I explain to the whole team tomorrow instead?"

"Okay," she said. I tried to decipher if it was "okay" as in "yes," "good," "I understand," or "if that's the best you can do." Or if it was just "okay." That Ukrainian okay was so versatile.

I chewed on the question a little at dinner at the restaurant I'd started going to after work, an Italian place across the street from my apartment in the city center. It was a small space with modern brick and wood décor, and food that was much closer to home than any of the other restaurants I'd tried in Ukraine. I'd intended to jot down some notes, but I was quickly so distracted by the presence of other patrons who could be watching me that I ended up writing fake notes, which looked like work, instead of doing the real work of thinking, which looked like doing nothing. Between fake notes, I had a fantastic bruschetta appetizer, a bottle of Belgian wheat beer, a bottle of mineral water, and a creamy and bacon-filled pasta carbonara, all for eleven dollars, including an extremely generous, by Ukrainian standards, 20 percent tip. I felt the lightness and freedom of wealth—of how little that money mattered to me and how guilt-free it felt to spend it. I wondered if rich people felt like this all the time or if it wore off.

After dinner, I crossed Prospekt Voli, the main street of the city center, which was busy during the day but quieted down at night, and turned into the courtyard that my pre-war apartment building shared with four other buildings. It was just after ten, a slight chill in the air, and leaves were falling from the trees as if to remind me that winter was coming. I said hello to the two puffy stray dogs that lived in the courtyard. The strays here were friendly, healthy looking, and omnipresent, trotting down streets and parks happy and unbothered. Apparently, Animal Control caught them, vaccinated and tagged them, and then released them back into the wild. I pressed the code on the analog pad on my building's front door, holding the three buttons down at the same time to pop open the lock. I walked the five flights of stairs to the top floor. As I reached the landing, I heard yelling coming from the other apartment on my floor.

I had yet to meet, or see, the neighbors. They sounded like a man and a woman, a married couple, maybe middle-aged, but it was hard to tell. Ukrainians speaking Ukrainian had much deeper voices than Americans. My first week in Lutsk, I'd heard a man in the market say something about bread in a flat baritone and looked down to see a child of maybe seven speaking. Regardless of how old my neighbors were, they sounded very upset—almost violent. I waited outside the door and listened for a minute, hoping there was no trouble. The yelling died down a little, so I went inside and let it be.

My apartment was a big one-bedroom with high ceilings, nice views of the park, and a price tag that, even with the Airbnb markup, was less than $400 per month. There were a few quirks—the wallpaper was gold and the elaborately carved moldings were actually Styrofoam. But compared to the listings I'd scoured before arriving, it was a find. Ukrainian housing sites had pages upon pages of photographs that looked like they were taken on nineties film showing suffocatingly furnished apartments: ancient armoires, dusty chairs, and old couches filling every inch of the room. In each photo, thick curtains sealed off the windows. American landlords tried to exaggerate the light coming into their apartment, but Ukrainians seemed intent on showing how completely it could be kept out. Thankfully, I had found this one apartment that had "European-style" decorating—a Ukrainian term for anything close to modern aesthetics.

Attached to the living room was a sun balcony that got too hot in September but was now, in October, a pleasant spot for a cup of coffee in the morning. The balcony offered a peekaboo view of Lubart's Castle, an unintentionally asymmetrical fort built by the Poles in the fourteenth century, which was Lutsk's biggest tourist attraction. Through the bedroom window, I could see the buses chugging along Prospekt Voli, the massive statue of the poet Taras Shevchenko in front of the university, and the fountain at the entrance to the park where teenagers posed for pictures.

I sat down with my laptop at the kitchen table and typed: *Ukrainians don't need small talk because . . .* But then I remembered my audience and started again: *Americans need small talk because . . .*

Because America is a diverse country—a country built by immigrants. That was always a good place to start. Ukraine was not diverse like America—about 95 percent of the population was ethnically Ukrainian, Russian, or both, and you could often go a full day here without seeing a person of color. Americans looked different from one another, and small talk helped us demonstrate that we meant no harm. Ukrainians didn't need small talk because they didn't fear one another. But that theory didn't hold. Germany, for example, was far more diverse than Ukraine, yet Germans were famously baffled by American-style small talk. Also, Ukraine was technically still engulfed in civil war in the east, albeit one orchestrated by Russia, which meant that at least some Ukrainians must fear one another.

I got up and walked a few laps around the apartment in search of a new theory. Maybe the difference in the role of the family in America as compared to Ukraine created a need for small talk among Americans that Ukrainians didn't share. Ukrainians spent much more time with their families, especially extended families, than Americans did, and maybe the widespread loneliness of American life meant that Americans had to find human contact outside of the home. Americans could scratch the loneliness itch, at least temporarily, through small talk.

Or maybe it was simpler. Ukraine had the legacy of the KGB to contend with. The threat of gulags could really discourage shooting the breeze, even decades later. Ukrainians grew up knowing that one mistake, one comment to a neighbor or a stranger about something as inconsequential as a movie or a radio station, could make your parents disappear. Every interaction outside the home was potentially a test. Why trust anyone outside your household? Why take any more risks than you needed to? It didn't matter that my call center agents had not grown up with these actual dangers—they grew up with their parents' memories of the dangers.

It was getting well past midnight, and with my brain starting to slow, I was nowhere closer to finding an answer. I decided to try again in the morning. But I found once my head had settled into the pillow, my brain wouldn't turn off. It needed to catalog my mistakes before it could sign off for the day.

My bedtime mistake auditing had first started tormenting me when I was ten. Maureen had theorized that it was because I blamed myself for my parents splitting, but that had happened two years earlier, so I didn't see the connection. Whatever it was that brought it on, it made it so that every time I started to drift into sleep I'd be woken by a jolt of regret. After several jolts, I'd think I was never going to fall asleep and start crying. Some nights, I'd cry and cry, thinking it would never end, until I would wake up in the morning and realize that it had ended. But many nights, my dad would hear me crying and bring me out into the kitchen. He'd set up a travel chessboard with plastic pieces for us to play. It was odd, at first, since neither of us really liked chess. But later I would suspect that was why my dad chose it: the dullness was calming.

As we moved the pieces across the board, my dad would ask what was wrong. I would shrug and say I didn't know. It felt shameful to feel so ashamed. But one night, for whatever reason, I told him: I couldn't sleep because I kept thinking about all the bad things I'd done. Then I listed them. The only one that I still remembered was that I picked a California poppy in our neighbor's yard, which we'd been told in school was illegal, since the state flower was protected. That wasn't technically true, but I didn't know it at the time.

"Oh, that?" he'd said. "That happens to me all the time."

He explained that the brain remembers mistakes more than triumphs because, from an evolutionary perspective, mistakes are what can kill you. Your brain is programmed to remind you of the things you did wrong.

Remember when you ate that red berry and vomited for eight hours? the brain asked the caveman. *Don't eat that berry again.*

Remember when you rustled the twigs and the saber-tooth chased you through the woods? Don't rustle the twigs.

"Even if we don't need to remember our mistakes like our ancestors did, our brains don't know that," my dad said. "So they keep telling us: *Don't mess up again. Don't mess up again.* But messing up is a part of life. If we're too scared to make mistakes, we can miss out on so much." He paused. "Besides, we're not even qualified to judge what was or wasn't a mistake until we get some distance to look back. Maybe the flower you picked was carrying a terrible disease that would have poisoned the tree in Mrs. Fisher's yard and brought it crashing down on her house. We don't know."

It was such a relief to hear him say that it was normal—that there was nothing wrong with me.

Tonight, as I lay awake, my brain was saying: *Remember when you made that joke at Sarah's birthday party and nobody laughed and it was just* quiet*? Don't do that again.*

Remember when you told Kyle that he needed to control his emotions better after a customer belittled him, basically taking the customer's side? Don't do that again.

Remember when Dad called and you didn't pick up because you were tired and weren't in the mood to talk politics, and then he died in his sleep? Don't do that again.

As these thoughts piled on top of one another, it occurred to me, as it had been occurring to me very often and very uselessly since my dad died, that no matter what I did, I, too, would eventually die. It was a very frustrating thought not only because it felt impossible to comprehend that existence would continue without my consciousness there to frame it, but because I couldn't talk to anyone about it. It was so clichéd and boring to be suddenly terrified at the realization that something that happened to everyone would also happen to you. What made it worse, though, was that my friends didn't seem to know how to talk about death, especially not my father's death, and because of this, they had either avoided the topic or avoided me altogether. It was like they were more scared of saying the wrong thing than of saying nothing.

Even Maureen would say, in a soothing tone, "It's okay if you don't want to talk about it." As if I was the one who didn't want to talk about it! I had to admit that the cracks in our relationship had been surfacing before all that, but after my dad died was when it got bad. What else was there to talk about? The greatest, most final ending there was had arrived, totally unexpectedly, to the person you loved the most, in the middle of the night, and maybe you cried and *let it all out* for a day or two—but then you weren't allowed to say anything about it? Or you could talk about it for a second until the other person said, *If you ever need to talk about it, I'm here for you.* As if that wasn't what you were already doing. As if, by interrupting you to say that they were there for you, they weren't showing that the exact opposite was true. Was it strange, then, when Americans couldn't talk about the things we so badly needed to talk about, that we had so much to say about the weather?

But just then, my thoughts were interrupted by the sound of the neighbors. They were arguing again, but this time I could hear them all the way through my bedroom wall. The arguing escalated. The man was now yelling at full volume. It sounded like there was going to be violence. But I'd misinterpreted many sights, smells, and sounds since moving to Ukraine. The fuck-you looks I'd seen on my first days in Kyiv were actually just a neutral expression. The smell of a gas leak, I'd learned, much to my embarrassment after my Airbnb host called the gas company and they sent out an inspector, was actually just the paint drying in the hallway of the apartment building. The sound of Ukrainian arguing that I was hearing now could actually just be a conversation. I tried to ignore it.

But then there was a thud. A punch. A cry. A woman gasping. I froze in the darkness, as if not moving would make it go away. I stood up. I sat back down. I stood up. I could run over there and pound on the door. But what would I say? I couldn't even speak the language. But what if he was still hitting her? She was gasping—what if she couldn't breathe? What if he was killing her?

I googled "number for police in Lutsk" and then translated the phrase "attack at Prospekt Voli, woman hurt, need help" and quickly repeated the phrase until I had it memorized. But then I heard the man's voice speaking softly, urgently, like he was comforting a child. The voices were close, as if they were leaning against the wall. I heard the woman crying and the man making apologetic sounds and speaking in a soft voice. Then the woman saying something. Then it sounded like they were crying together.

I didn't know what to do. The man had hit her. I should call the police. But if I called the police, what would happen? Would they arrest him? Or would they just show up, decide no crime had been committed, then leave him there with her, empowered and maybe even angrier than before?

My body spent all night releasing chemicals designed to make me do *something*—fight or flight. But I didn't call the cops. I didn't go next door. I just paced around worrying and searched the internet for answers.

When I finally fell asleep, I fell too asleep, overslept, and woke in the afternoon to the sound of the woman next door. She was talking loudly, but in a conversational voice, seemingly undistressed, and the lack of another voice made me think she was on the phone. It sounded like she was okay, despite my inaction. I had learned while late-night googling that the Ukrainian parliament had only passed a bill criminalizing domestic violence in late 2017. Which meant that up to last year, it would have been legal for my neighbor to hit his wife. She'd been on her own for a long time, I'd rationalized—what good would me trying to swoop in have done? Maybe doing nothing had been the right thing. More likely, I was being a coward. But I couldn't dwell—I had to rush to get ready so that I'd have enough time at the office to prep my still-unwritten lecture on small talk.

I turned on the shower, but nothing came out of the showerhead. I checked the kitchen faucet; it wasn't working either. I wasn't sure if there was a switch I had to reset or a Ukrainian water company to call. But I hadn't fallen asleep until after sunrise and I was too tired to solve it. I tried to blow-dry and deodorant myself into presentability.

At the office, I hadn't been at my desk for more than five minutes when Dima came by to ask if I would like to have some coffee. Since that first day he let me into the office, Dima and I hadn't talked for more than a few sentences total—the end of his shift was the beginning of mine—but when I came into the office he always stopped what he was doing to say hello and shake my hand. And I had been going by John ever since.

"I would love some coffee," I told him. My head was starting to crack and I was already regretting the decision to skip my coffee at home. Sometimes I would convince myself that I didn't actually need something—I just thought I did. And then, when faced with the absence of the thing I convinced myself I didn't need, I would find that I did need it.

I followed Dima and three of the other developers—most of whom I'd never spoken with but had wordlessly shaken hands with many times, as seemed to be the custom for Ukrainian men—to the kitchen upstairs. While I didn't know the developers, I knew of them from Facebook, which was apparently still very popular in Ukraine, as I had been friended by everyone in the office except for Natalie. Of the developers, I knew that Maxim posted intellectual think pieces, Serhii posted prank videos, and Igor posted Chelsea FC content. But the pages I'd spent the most time on were those of the agents.

Lisa, the quietest of the agents, a woman with short dark hair who wore polo shirts to work, had immediately endeared herself to me by being the only person in the office who wore glasses. In person she was shy, looking down whenever I tried to talk with her, and I hadn't gotten to know her at all. But on Facebook, her page showed that she had once been an aspiring photographer. A dewdrop clung to a flower petal in black and white. A handprint stained a kitchen window, blurring the sun behind it. There were several images from a few years back of her crowded into the frame with other black-clad Ukrainian hipsters. Her newer pictures were all of a cute baby girl with chubby cheeks and a thoroughly un-Ukrainian smile. Angie was apparently a mother of two, which I never would have guessed, given that she dressed more like a child than a mother. But she frequently posted portraits with her husband and sons that looked professionally done—the four of them sitting on a picnic blanket with lighting so perfect it must have been artificial. Kyle and Andy posted pretty much what you would expect of twenty-one-year-old boys—links to livestreams of people playing video games and jokes that lost something when I hit the translate button. But there were older pictures of Kyle huddled into the frame with friends in the main square of Wrocław and of Andy playing acoustic guitar on a camping trip in the Carpathians. I couldn't have pictured the agents' outside-the-office lives based on their work personas, but after I'd learned of them, it made their work selves feel more in need of protection, as those selves were no longer their whole being but simply what they did to sustain the rest of their selves. The only agent who hadn't friended me was Natalie, and it didn't feel appropriate for me to friend her—almost like a professor friending a student—so she remained in-real-life only.

Dima worked the espresso machine and handed out little paper cups. Out the kitchen window, across a run-down two-lane road, I watched the Styr River flowing through an overgrown field, pulling fallen branches downstream. Serhii asked Maxim something in Ukrainian, and Maxim admonished him, probably reminding him that the American didn't speak Ukrainian. Which was kind. But the result was five men leaning on counters and drinking in silence.

Finally, Maxim, who was a shorter guy in his thirties, asked me in halting English what city I was from.

I answered in slow, clear, and what I hoped was friendly English that I had lived in a city called Portland, but that I was born in Los Angeles. Maxim asked if it was hot in Los Angeles. I smiled and said,

"Yes, you're right! It's sunny almost every day, the whole year. It's twenty degrees and sunny even on Christmas."

After that first question landed, the others followed in quick succession.

Igor wanted to know if it was true that many Americans borrowed to buy their homes. Dima wanted to know the average rent in Los Angeles. Serhii, an older guy, was the only one who stuck to Ukrainian, asking Dima to translate. Dima asked me for Serhii what the interest rates for borrowing in America were; my answer, going off their reactions, was shockingly low.

"What do Americans think about Ukraine?" Igor said.

"I don't think Americans know much about Ukraine, to be honest," I said. "Unfortunately, we can be ignorant when it comes to other countries."

"But why should you know about Ukraine? It's very far away," Maxim said, with what I thought was an abundance of understanding. I had a hard time imagining thinking it perfectly normal for foreigners to be ignorant of your country. "But tell me, please," Maxim continued, "do you believe that there are misconceptions in America about Ukraine?"

The way he said the word "misconceptions" sounded like he was trying it out for the first time. I wanted to give him a hug.

"That's a very good question," I said. A misconception required first a conception, and I wasn't sure how many Americans had any conception of Ukraine. Of those who knew of Ukraine, I suspected that many thought it was part of Russia. A lot of Americans still called the country the Ukraine instead of just Ukraine, even though that hadn't been correct since 1991. Ukraine literally meant "borderland"; when Ukraine was part of the Soviet Union, it was the borderland to Europe. But since 1991, it was no longer the borderland.

"Americans tend to spell 'Kyiv' the Russian way, *K-i-e-v*," I said.

Maxim nodded. “I understand.”

Ten minutes later, I felt—though I might have just been projecting—that everyone was buoyed by how we had all conducted such a successful conversation in English. I had forgotten about all the anxiety and terribleness with the neighbors the night before, and I was ready to write my small-talk talk now. But when the developers filed out toward the door to return to work, Dima stopped me.

“Would you like another Americano, John?”

“I’d love one.”

Ukrainian coffee was bad, and the espresso from this machine was particularly rank—both watery and acidic at the same time. But it was coffee, with a colleague, which was something I was happy to indulge for another cup.

“Do you know why they call it an Americano?” I said as he worked the machine. I explained that, during World War II, American soldiers in Italy had wanted American-style coffee, drip coffee, which hadn’t existed at the time in Italy—and still did not exist in Ukraine. So the Italians started pouring hot water in the espressos to make them more like American coffee.

Dima laughed. “I think LA is maybe my city. I would like to go there one day.”

“I think you would like it there,” I said.

“Tell me, John,” Dima said as he handed me my coffee. “Are you married?”

“I am not.”

“Why not?”

“I don’t know exactly. I was dating a girl for a few years. But it didn’t work out.”

“Why did it not work out?” Dima said, searching for the “w” in “work” through an abundant exhalation.

"I'm not sure why." I took a sip. "What about you? Are you married?"

"No. But I know why I'm not married. It was my fault. I made too many mistakes and the girl did not want me anymore. This is the great tragedy of my life. I cannot get her back. No one will be as good as her."

"Oh, I'm sorry."

"But," Dima said, his voice brightening, "the other way to see it is that she taught me how to love. The next time a good girl comes along, I will be able to value the relationship. But tell me, please, John: Is Amazon popular in America?"

The free jazz of Ukrainian conversation no longer surprised me. I told him that Amazon was extremely popular in America, and that a good percentage of the products sold to American consumers were sold on Amazon.

Dima said that was great!

I wasn't sure it was great, but I wasn't going to stop the momentum of the conversation.

"I sell earplugs on Amazon in America," Dima said.

"Really?"

Dima explained that he was the founder and owner of the ninth-best-selling earplug brand on Amazon. "But I hope to be number one, one day."

"How did you get into that?"

Dima said that he had borrowed money from two friends to take a course on how to find a niche in the American market.

"I received a list of two hundred markets that someone with my level of capital might be able to break into. But I wanted to find a market that I could not only break into, but also build a presence in for several months before I began to show profits. I kept crossing products off that were financially impossible until there was only one product left. Earplugs."

Dima said that, at the time, he had never heard of earplugs and had to look up what they were. But now he couldn't imagine his life without them.

"They are awesome! If you live by a road and cars are going crazy, or if you're in a hostel and someone is coming home late at night, or if you just want quiet, earplugs are very useful."

I said that I'd been using earplugs for years.

"So you know!"

Deciding to lean into the rhythm of the conversation, I asked Dima about the water situation in my apartment and whether I should call the landlord.

"How long has the water been broken?"

"Just today."

"Then it's no problem. It will be back tonight, maybe tomorrow."

"It's good that I asked. If this was America, I would have called the second the water didn't come out of the faucet."

"Yes! I have heard Oksana explain this to the agents. They say, 'Why do the customers call about this? It's not even a big problem!' And she says, 'Because Americans always call! You must understand! For every problem, Americans call!'"

"It's a big difference between Americans and Ukrainians, I gather."

"Slavic people, they try every possible thing before they call for help."

"That's probably a better way of doing it."

"Maybe. Maybe not. If Americans didn't call for help, none of the agents here would have jobs. Or maybe there would be one agent instead of five. And they are paid well." He said that the agents earned a salary that I calculated as a little over five dollars per hour. I hadn't realized they made so much less than the developers. "With this much money, they can make it rain," Dima said, and mimed flicking bills off his palm.

I laughed, partly because Dima was trying to be funny and partly from the shock of hearing someone who's not fluent using slang. I looked at my watch. The agents would be arriving for their shift soon, and I still had to figure out what I was going to say about small talk. But there was still one big question on my mind, and Dima had presented me with an unexpected opportunity to ask someone who might have the answer. I felt a familiar tightening of my skin when I had to say something uncomfortable. All of a sudden my teeth felt too big for my mouth.

"Dima, could I ask one more piece of advice?"

"Yes, of course."

"Here in Ukraine—or, here in Lutsk, I should say. Here in Lutsk, is it normal here for men to hit women?"

Dima waited. "I don't understand."

"If you saw a man hit a woman, would you call the police?"

"Where did you see this?"

"I didn't see it. I heard it in my apartment."

"Someone attacked a woman in your apartment?"

"My neighbors. The husband hit his wife."

"Oh." He paused.

"Should I call the police?"

"The police, they do not do this. It is not their job. If there is a child in the home, there is a service for that that you can call. But it's not the police."

"I don't think there's a child."

"Then . . ." Dima appeared to look for the words but eventually just shrugged.

"So there's nothing I can do?"

"I don't know." He looked at his watch. "We should return to the office."

Not only had I failed to learn what I should do, but I had offended Dima, who, up until that point, had seemed like he might be my friend. I didn't have any friends in Ukraine yet, and until now I hadn't realized how much I would have liked one.

But as we walked down the stairs, Dima turned back to me and said, "Tell me, please, John, do you like big tennis?"

"Big tennis?"

"Like Roger Federer."

"Oh, I see. What's little tennis, then?"

"Tennis on a table."

"In America, we call that tennis and table tennis."

"Table tennis," he repeated.

"I don't really know anything about tennis."

"Boxing?"

"I like boxing," I said, meaning that I liked to watch boxing sometimes.

"Then maybe one day we will do boxing. They have a good place here. It's awesome."

"Sounds great."

"Okay." Dima opened the door to the office.

"It was really nice talking with you, Dima."

"Yes. Really nice talking with you, John." Dima repeated the phrase—"really nice talking with you"—to himself a few times as he returned to his desk.

I spent the next half hour frantically typing up notes. But there wasn't enough time. The agents settled into their desks, and I began the talk without knowing how it would end.

"Yesterday Natalie pointed out something very important." I looked over at Natalie, expecting to see her blush, look down, nod, or react in some way. But her expression didn't change. She was wearing a gray sweater with a silver necklace and silver earrings, and that subtle application of makeup that looks like no makeup. I had to stop looking. "I've been teaching you *how* Americans small-talk, but not *why* Americans small-talk. It's very difficult to master something without knowing why you're doing it. That was a mistake on my part. So, let's brainstorm here. Why do you think Americans want to small-talk?"

"Americans—" Oksana began.

"Oksana, I'm asking the agents. Please quietly observe." Employing the Ukrainian directness felt horrible. I intentionally didn't look at Oksana; if she looked hurt, I wouldn't have been able to stop myself from softening. "Kyle, what do you think?"

Kyle's face was expressionless. "I don't know."

"He is asking for you to try!" Oksana said. At least she wasn't discouraged.

"If you were to guess, Kyle," I said, "what would you say? There are no wrong answers. Why do you think Americans like small talk?"

"Maybe they are bored."

"Very good. I think that's part of it." I took an easel with a pad of paper that sat in the corner, brought it over, and wrote: *Bored.* "What else? Angie?"

"Yes?"

"Why do you think Americans like to small-talk?"

"Maybe they are trying to get a better price. Maybe they think we can give them a better price if they are kind to us."

"That's very possible. Let's write that down." I wrote: *Want a better deal.* When I turned back, I saw, to my happy surprise, a raised hand. But it was Andy's hand—a sign that a teachable moment was on the horizon.

"Maybe they have no families, so they want to talk to us, even though they have never met us."

I was surprised at how close Andy had gotten to one of my own theories of small talk from the night before.

"That's very insightful, Andy. Let's write it down." *Lonely.* "What about you, Natalie?" I said. "What do you think?"

"I don't know. I have never been to America."

"We're just brainstorming. Take a guess?"

"You are the only American here, so maybe we should ask you. Why do *you* like small talk, John?"

I noticed Dima look over from his developer's desk.

"I think it's comforting," I said. "You get to talk to another person without any risks. Since you're not talking about anything important, there's no chance to say the wrong thing."

"But why does it matter if you say the wrong thing?" Natalie said.

"Maybe it shouldn't matter. But it does matter—to me at least. When I say the wrong thing, I feel bad about it for a long time. Don't you feel bad about it when you say the wrong thing?"

"Yes," Dima said from his desk. "It keeps me from sleeping at night."

"Thank you, Dima. But what about you, Natalie? Do you feel bad when you say the wrong thing?"

She shrugged. "Maybe. Maybe not. There are worse things a person can do."

"That's true." I waited, but Natalie was apparently done. "What about this one?" I wrote on the paper: *Something to do while waiting.* "What do we think of this one?"

After a pause, Lisa, who never volunteered an answer, adjusted her glasses and chimed in, much to my delight. "Frankly speaking, I believe it's very difficult for them to wait."

"Absolutely, Lisa! We Americans are like children. We're used to getting everything immediately. When we're waiting, we want to be entertained." I wrote: *Entertainment*.

"But how is talking about the weather entertaining?" Natalie said. She seemed angry, but that was a feeling I often got when Ukrainians asked questions.

I thought about it for a moment. "Do you ever take walks?"

"Certainly," Natalie said.

"Do you only take walks to places you need to go?"

"I don't understand."

"Do you only walk when you have to do something—to go to the supermarket, the bakery, the office? Or do you ever walk just to walk? Do you ever just stroll around the park, Old Town, or the city center?"

"Sometimes I walk just to walk."

"And if you're walking just to walk, does it matter where you're going?"

"How do you mean?"

"Is there a destination you have to reach? Or is the purpose of the walk the walk itself?"

"In this situation, the purpose is the walk itself."

"Exactly. In the same way, in small talk, the purpose isn't the information communicated—it's the talk itself. When you take a walk, you're stretching your legs and exercising your body, looking at the changing scenery, and generally interacting with the world around you. When you share some small talk, you're stretching your vocal cords, exercising your mind, and interacting with the world around you—even if you can't see it over the phone—by talking with another person." I looked for signs of understanding in the agents' faces but saw none. "Think of small talk as a 'small walk.' You're taking a little conversational walk with the customer to pass the time you have to spend waiting. Does that make sense?"

Nobody said anything.

"Does that make sense, Natalie?"

"Okay," she said. "I understand."

"Lisa? Kyle?"

They nodded.

I looked at the clock. Three fifty-nine.

"Okay, let's take some small walks!"

I strolled back to my desk, feeling light and bouncy. It had gone so well! They had learned something. At least I thought they had. Maybe they hadn't. But if nothing else, they had listened, responded, and likely understood at least part of what I was saying. I wanted to call my dad and tell him about how well it had gone, how much progress we were making. But then I remembered, first, the time difference—how it wasn't yet 6:00 a.m. in California—and, second, how he was dead.

A FEW EVENINGS LATER, WALKING HOME FROM WORK, I GOT AN email from Gene, the partner at my dad's firm—while there were two names on the letterhead, there was only one partner, since the other partner, Gene's brother, hadn't been heard from in twelve years and my dad had repeatedly turned down a partnership on account of it was too much trouble—inviting me to attend a ceremony naming the conference room after my dad. Gene's was a small workers' comp firm run out of the back unit of a suburban office park where I'd file-clerked as a teenager, and he'd always been kind to me. I was touched by the gesture, not because it was so great to have a shabby little conference room that no one used named after you, but because it showed that Gene was still thinking about my dad almost a year after he died.

I wrote Gene to thank him. *But unfortunately, I won't be able to attend, since I recently moved to Ukraine for work.* The funeral had already been too much. I'd been so angry. At the secretary who'd had the audacity to laugh about a story unrelated to my dad at the reception, at my dad's cousin who kept starting sentences with "What you don't understand about your father," at Maureen for no good reason. The only person whom I hadn't been angry at that day had been Gene, who had cried a little bit in a way that felt sincere instead of performative. I felt guilty at how relieved I was to have an excuse to not attend

Gene's ceremony. But I couldn't go through all that again, even if it had been geographically possible.

Just minutes later, before I'd even gotten home, Gene sent a reply.

Sorry to hear that, maybe you want to write something about your dad to have read at the ceremony? -G

After that short message were eight lines of text stating that this email was PRIVILEGED AND CONFIDENTIAL and copying or redistributing by non-intended recipient was STRICTLY PROHIBITED. I flashed back to getting emails from my dad like, *Wow the Clippers really suck* followed by the same PRIVILEGED AND CONFIDENTIAL warning.

I was a trained journalist—it shouldn't be that hard to write something. But the thought of starting filled me with dread. I'd been writing in one form or another for as long as I could remember, but I'd already used a story about my dad encouraging my writing in my eulogy. When I was fifteen, I'd showed him my first editorial for the school newspaper, "Is It Whack to Attack Iraq?," and he'd said that I made some really good points that may have been slightly undermined by the headline. It was a good eulogy story because it showed his gentleness and his honesty. I didn't mention that he'd always wanted to be a writer but had given up on that dream for practicality's sake. Instead, I used the story to highlight the side of him that everyone knew—his ease with people, his competence in almost all situations—while giving away a few, but not too many, of the private memories I had left. And it was also short and funny. It was so difficult to condense a lifetime of love into little funny stories, but the alternative was platitudes that could have been true about anyone.

He used to say that it was the distance between what you wanted and what you had that made you unhappy. By that logic, if I stopped wanting to be a journalist I'd stop being unhappy about it. But thinking about it as I crossed Prospekt Voli, I wasn't totally sure that my dad had been the one who said it. It was getting harder and harder to remember what he'd said and how he'd said it. I remembered how the things he said made me feel or how I interpreted the things he said. But that wasn't the same as remembering *what* he'd said. I regularly rewatched a short video I'd taken of him trying to tell a joke but laughing too hard to get to the punch line, because I feared I might forget what his laughter sounded like. But I didn't have a video of him saying the thing about the distance between what you wanted and what you had, and I suspected it may have actually come from a mindfulness app I'd been using lately.

He would've liked it here, I thought, as I walked the 102 stairs to my apartment, which I could finally climb without getting out of breath. He would've said things like, *I wonder what it was like under Khrushchev.* He would've told me lots of Cold War history that I didn't know—maybe Ukrainian history I didn't know. He would've continued calling it the Ukraine even after I told him to drop the article. He wasn't one to be told what to do. He would've liked Dima. He would've liked Natalie. But he liked, or at least got along with, pretty much everyone. I thought about sending that to Gene—*my dad liked everybody*—but it sounded so generic that it made me angry. Then, before I knew it, the anger filled me completely, and it was all I could do to keep from punching the door.

I sat down on the couch, did some breathing exercises, repeated to myself that it was okay to be feeling whatever I was feeling, and then smiled in wonder at how unspecial I was that saying something that lame and cliché actually calmed me down. I wrote to Gene saying that I was swamped with my new job and that I didn't think I would be able to come up with anything befitting the memory of my dad before the ceremony. Then I closed the window and began sketching out a draft of a satisfaction survey that we could start sending customers. But I kept refreshing my email, hoping Gene would write back saying not to worry about it—they didn't need my words. The more minutes passed without that message, the guiltier I felt.

My dad wasn't perfect. He could be an incredible pain in the ass, no more so than when he felt the need to needle you and push your buttons for no discernible reason. He liked to play devil's advocate all the time. He could get irritated at you for things that weren't your fault, like if you caught a cold. But he was also a good person who was always there for me. He was someone who started volunteering for an immigration and civil rights nonprofit when he was sixty-seven after decades of political apathy because he saw people in trouble. Instead of just complaining about what was going on, he actually used his skills to help, not in a glamorous way, but by proofreading briefs for younger lawyers with more expertise on the subject, looking up case law, and getting everyone lunch.

I couldn't write about that, though, because then the whole thing would just break into a political argument instead of a celebration of my dad. Even having told Gene I wouldn't be contributing, I couldn't stop thinking about it. By three in the morning, it felt important to just say *something*—even if it wasn't the right thing.

I wrote out a story about the time a neighbor of ours—the landlord's son who lived in a trailer on the vacant lot next door—came over and asked my dad if he could borrow sixty dollars to take his daughter to Chuck E. Cheese for her birthday. His paycheck wasn't coming until Friday, the neighbor explained, and his daughter's mom was supposed to take her, but she had appendicitis, so they'd switched days. My dad was normally a hard-ass when he smelled bullshit and it was pretty clear the neighbor had a drug problem, so I was surprised when my dad gave him the money and said, "Tell her happy birthday for me."

After he left, I told my dad the neighbor was lying.

"Maybe," my dad said. "Maybe not. But if a man needs to come over to ask his neighbor for sixty dollars for his daughter, then he probably needs the money—whatever he needs it for."

"What if he spends it on drugs?"

"Then I imagine he's going to have a great time at Chuck E. Cheese."

The story was supposed to show how kind he could be when kindness was needed. But on paper, I worried that it made him look gullible, especially to a roomful of lawyers. I deleted it and started over.

My dad knew right from wrong, I finally wrote, cringing. *He prosecuted liars and frauds without remorse. I never saw him laugh harder than when he told the story of the PI he sent to follow a plaintiff who supposedly had such a severe spinal injury that he couldn't walk. But when the plaintiff saw the PI, he got so mad that he chased him down the street, threatening to kill him—all on camera.*

That would almost certainly get a laugh.

But he was also never afraid to help people who needed help. He did pro bono work for clients who were so injured and spiritually broken that they couldn't help themselves, and took years of their complaining phone calls with patience and generosity. They didn't realize what a great job he was doing for them, and he felt no need to tell them. He told me that it wasn't them yelling at him—it was the pain. He helped them without expecting so much as a thank-you in return. He helped them because it was the right thing to do. I closed my eyes and hit send.

I DIDN'T HEAR MY NEIGHBORS AGAIN UNTIL THE FOLLOWING week. I was on the couch after work, streaming the Ukrainian sitcom *Servant of the People*, about a schoolteacher who's elected president through a write-in campaign after a video of him ranting against corruption goes viral, and just fading into that lovely state where your mind starts loosening its grip—the subtitles started to blur, and I was holding a woman's hand, and her hand turned to water, but I didn't find it strange—when the neighbors started yelling. I sat up. Suddenly everything was very real again. The man was yelling words I didn't understand peppered with a few I did. "But now," he said, and then some other things. "Never!" he said.

"But why?" the woman said, in a voice more exasperated than angry. "Not good," she said, and then lots of other words.

They argued for almost an hour in a way that would have been more annoying than scary were it not for the memory of last time. Even after they went quiet, I was on high alert, and every shifting creak in the bed frame, every dropped bottle outside, and every step in the stairwell yanked me right out of sleep. By morning, though the argument had never escalated past words, I was exhausted from the effort of making myself fall asleep so many times.

At the office, I got lost in the notes I was typing up for an agent-led workshop where they would critique one another's calls, and when I looked up, almost all the day-shift developers had left for lunch. A cleaning woman in her forties with short blond hair was mopping and wiping down surfaces. She motioned to my desk to ask if she could clean it.

"*Bud' laska*," I said, which meant both "please" and "you're welcome," but the way she looked at me suggested that I had said neither.

Before arriving, I had convinced myself that I would pick up Ukrainian quickly out of necessity, since Ukrainians didn't speak much English. Until recently, they hadn't had much use for it. The country's long economic relationship with Russia rather than the EU, the prohibitive cost of and difficulty obtaining visas to travel west, the lack of European tourism to Ukraine, and the widespread corruption that discouraged foreign investment meant that Ukrainians hadn't been incentivized to learn English like people in the EU countries. But then the revolution came. In late 2013, a few hundred students had gathered at Maidan—Kyiv's main square—to protest the corrupt pro-Russian government's last-minute pullout from a deal to bring Ukraine closer to the EU. Ukrainians were used to the government letting them down, and, at least according to the books I'd read and videos I'd watched before leaving, they had a seemingly endless capacity for shrugging off the world's unfairness. This latest disappointment might not have been any different from the others had the government not sent in the police to attack the students. The videos of police attacking the protesters at Maidan—especially of them beating teenage girls—had been a push too far.

The day after the police charged the students, half a million Ukrainians took to Maidan to protest. And they stayed. Demonstrators camped out on the square for months. The movement grew, and the protesters refused to relent, even when the winter turned dismally cold, when police sent snipers to the rooftops to open fire, or when government-hired thugs started kidnapping, torturing, and murdering protesters or supporters caught driving them supplies. By spring 2014, the Maidan Revolution had toppled the corrupt pro-Russian government, sent the president fleeing to Russia, and brought a pro-European government to power. Russia had used the chaos of revolution and regime change to invade Ukrainian Crimea and start a war in Eastern Ukraine. But though Russia took Crimea, the war in the east had been fought to a standstill, and Ukraine had, in many ways, recovered.

Now Ukraine was desperately trying to become a part of Europe—a difficult proposition, since a combination of Russian disinformation about Ukraine and the real corruption that still plagued the new Ukrainian government made EU countries hesitant to offer membership—and suddenly English was a commodity. Only about 20 percent of Ukrainians could speak English at all, compared with over 60 percent in neighboring Poland, which had fallen into the EU sphere of influence rather than Russia's. I had found English hard to come by in Kyiv, but that was nothing compared to Lutsk, where it felt like all the city's English speakers worked at my office. If I wanted to have a full life in Ukraine, I would have to learn the language. But Ukrainian, it turned out, was really hard.

To further complicate things, there was more than one language spoken in Ukraine, a bilingual country split between Ukrainian and Russian. In Kyiv, there seemed to be a pretty even mix of Ukrainian and Russian, even though the city was, politically, anti-Russian. In Lutsk, the preferred language was Ukrainian. In both cities, both languages were spoken, and while the two were supposedly mutually intelligible to native speakers, neither was intelligible to me.

The Cyrillic alphabet had been much easier to learn than I'd expected—just a week or two of flash cards before I left Portland had done the trick. I remembered my first day in Kyiv, stopping on a corner near the national soccer stadium and sounding out bright red text over a storefront: ФОКСТРОТ. *F-o-k-s-t-r-o-t. Foxtrot.* The store was called Foxtrot! I had no idea what it sold. But it didn't matter. I could make the letters into sounds!

But in the weeks that followed, I hadn't made it much past just sounding out words. Pronunciation was hard, as Ukrainian had all kinds of sounds that I'd never encountered before. *Hry. Mno.* I knew that these arrangements of letters were accessible to me, since Ukrainians with the same mouth and lungs that I had conjured them without problems—I just didn't know how or where to find them. But the grammar was the worst. In Ukrainian, whenever anything changed in a sentence, it wasn't just the verb that needed conjugating but also the noun. It didn't help that Ukrainian had six cases.

I tried an online course in Ukrainian, but it was frontloaded with useless information about numbers and animals. Next, I tried a tutor Oksana recommended, an extremely focused graduate student who came to my apartment twice and taught by rote. We had to get every single detail 100 percent right before moving on, which meant that our two lessons were excruciating call-and-response sessions. Finally, I tried a new audio course that had been recommended on one of the message boards and was, as it turned out, the best thing on the market. The course moved at the right pace and taught phrases that actually had utility.

But for every three or four useful units, there was another unit that seemed geared to a specific clientele.

But wouldn't you like to have something to drink with me?

Maybe later?

At the hotel?

At your place?

Just like the message boards, it turned out that the language courses designed for men looking for sex were the most useful courses, even if I wasn't a man looking for sex. The pickup lines were uncomfortable. The vocabulary for haggling with sex workers—*I can give you money but not that much*—was worse. I was constantly reminded of the reason most men who looked like me came to Ukraine. But nevertheless, the language course worked better than anything else, and I soon found myself navigating my encounters with the grocery store cashiers, waitstaff, and cabdrivers with greater confidence.

When I tried out my Ukrainian at the office, both the agents and the developers were very encouraging of my halting attempts. Aside from Natalie, who would say things like, "Very good, John. If you continue like this, you will speak Ukrainian in ten years." Which I didn't mind at all.

Once, Serhii, who wasn't comfortable speaking English—and, as a developer, didn't need to—tried to teach me a Ukrainian phrase, but Dima intervened before I could repeat it.

"That means 'fuck you,'" Dima said.

I threw my hands up playfully. "This is no good, Serhii! I can't learn bad words."

"*Ale chomu?*" he said.

"Because when I get nervous, I mix up the Ukrainian words I know."

He didn't understand, so Dima translated.

"Like if I'm at the store," I went on. "When the cashier asks me if I have a membership card, I've learned that I'm supposed to say, '*Ni, ya ne mayu.*' But if I know how to say 'fuck you,' one day the cashier is going to say, 'Do you have a membership card?' and I'm going to say, 'Fuck you.' And that will not be good."

Serhii had laughed and said, "*Dobre dobre,*" meaning "okay okay" or possibly other affirmative words.

That afternoon, feeling both grateful that the cleaning lady had done such a nice job on my desk and guilty that I was benefiting from the labor of a cleaner—I had been so uncomfortable when she was cleaning my area that I went upstairs for a coffee—I wanted to thank her. But all of the developers were out to lunch except for Serhii. I debated whether it was worth asking for his help or if he would just mess with me. I finally walked over to his desk and asked him in Ukrainian if he could assist me.

"*Certainly*," he said, in Ukrainian.

I asked him how to say, "Thank you for cleaning my desk."

He squinted.

I mimed cleaning my desk and then said "thank you" in Ukrainian several times until Serhii understood.

"*Dobre, dobre*," he said. Then he gave me a difficult phrase: *zaymatysya seksom zi mnoyu*.

I tried it several times, and Serhii, with surprising patience for a man I'd marked as the class clown, helped me in the places where I'd slipped up, showing me how to shape my lips to elicit the sound, until I'd said the phrase so many times it would be imprinted in my brain forever. Just like in America, in Ukraine some men were simply kinder one-on-one, freed of the need to perform for the group. I thanked him and walked down to find the cleaning ladies on the ground floor. I was mumbling the sentence quietly on the stairs when I ran into Dima and Maxim returning from lunch.

"John, tell me please, what are you saying?" Dima asked.

I told him I was going to thank the cleaning lady for cleaning my desk.

Dima said that that wasn't necessary. "But if you are going to say thank you, maybe a different way? You are currently saying, 'Have sex with me.'"

I assured him that I was not saying that. *"Zaymatysya seksom zi mnoyu."*

"Yes, this means 'have sex with me.'"

I felt the heat flowing to my face.

I took the stairs two at a time and stormed over to Serhii's desk.

"Dima, tell Serhii that if he ever does that again, he's fired."

Dima looked at me. "I don't understand."

"This is a place of business. If he does that again, he's fired. Sacked. He will not work here anymore."

Dima was quiet for a minute. Then he said it in Ukrainian. Serhii said something back, sounding surprised. Dima said something to him that may or may not have been angry.

Then Serhii held up his hands as if in defeat. "Okay," he said in English. "Sorry. Joke."

"*Dobre*," I said, and returned to my desk.

It was quiet in the office for the rest of the day. At the end of their shift, the developers left, and the agents came in, but they also seemed uncomfortable, as if they'd gotten the memo that I'd completely lost my cool. Even Natalie, who always seemed to have a teasing word for me, was more formal and briefer than usual. I felt awful. Everyone hated me. But I was the boss. This was my job. At my desk, I must have replayed the scene a hundred times, but it only occurred to me after work, back at my apartment, that Serhii was a developer, not an agent. I couldn't fire him if I wanted to.

In search of a distraction, I flicked through the Ukrainian channels on the satellite dish I never used. I landed on *Friends* dubbed into Russian. I understood even less Russian than Ukrainian, but it didn't matter—I knew all the lines by heart, since Maureen and I often watched *Friends* before bed. Our own friends were always surprised to learn this, *Friends* being such a milquetoast and heteronormative show, but I loved the comfort and safety of its company, and the way you could talk through it without missing anything. Maureen and I would snack in bed and reminiscence about nineties clothes, Y2K hair, or the year when everyone got a spray tan.

One night, Maureen said she thought Chandler was maybe the most Gen X character in popular television. "His sarcasm is his defining characteristic. He has a punch line for everything. He's emotionally vacant and he uses other people's problems as an occasion to perform."

I said that I thought I would've been a good Gen Xer—the blissfully self-centered white guy with a sarcastic comment for every occasion. "Maybe I was just born fifteen years too late when we were expected to have feelings and stuff. Hey, stop stealing my M and M's. You said you didn't want me to get you any."

"*Our* M and M's," she said, and did a double head fake before trying again to steal the M&M's, and again being swatted away. "The idea that you would've been great at being Gen X shows that you wouldn't have been great at being Gen X, since Gen Xers don't say they want to be great at things. The correct Gen X response is 'whatever.' Now gimme candy."

"Good point," I said, and handed her the bowl.

"Besides, if you were born fifteen years earlier, the Gen X world might've let you stay adolescently one-dimensional forever."

"Not necessarily. I would've met you and blossomed into a three-dimensional person."

Maureen leaned over and kissed me. It was that kind of kiss that held no drama or promise of anything more, no hope for sex, and no risk of rejection. It was easy to forget about the calm contentment like that when you were in the middle of it. I turned off Russian *Friends*, got up, and went to bed.

When I came into the office the next day, I found Oksana sitting at my desk, grading papers. This was unusual; she normally didn't come in until the agents' shift started. My first thought was that taking my desk was an escalation in our pedagogic turf war of learn-by-doing versus learn-by-scolding. But then I realized the others must have asked her to speak to me about yesterday's incident with Serhii.

"Good afternoon, John." She pulled together her papers in one quick motion and placed them in a large leather purse. "Are you hungry?"

I didn't like that she was both waiting at my desk and the one making the lunch invitation. But I had come to accept that I would always be at a disadvantage with Oksana. One time she'd mentioned that her car wouldn't start that morning, and when I said that I was sorry, she looked at me like there was something wrong with me. What kind of person would be bothered by car trouble?

For lunch, she drove us in her Japanese mid-sized SUV back to Prospekt Voli. We drove past the big, white-pillared university building that I could see from my window.

"I teach English here," Oksana said.

It was an intimidating building. "It's a beautiful building."

"It used to be the Party headquarters for the region."

I learned that, in addition to teaching English at the university and the office, Oksana also gave weekend tours of Chernobyl and had three adult children. I said it sounded like she was busy.

"Please, we need a better word than 'busy,'" she said. "'Busy' is so overused."

We parked behind a car with a bumper sticker of a high-heel shoe on a red triangle that I'd seen occasionally on the streets of both Kyiv and Lutsk.

"What's the high heel mean?" I asked.

"It means that a woman is driving. So that you are more considerate of her."

"You don't have one on your car."

"No," she agreed.

We crossed the street in chilly afternoon sunlight and stepped into the same Italian restaurant where I had taken to eating my dinner five times a week. Oksana asked the hostess for one menu in English, but the hostess already had an English menu in her hand—though technically it was written in Italian, but it qualified as English since the characters were Latin rather than Cyrillic—having handed it to me many times before.

"My face must give me away," I explained to Oksana. I didn't want her to know how often I ate here, both because she was presenting me with something nice and because I didn't want her to know how much money I made. After the initial happy shock of the cheap Ukrainian prices had worn off, I'd realized that the carbonara at one of the fanciest restaurants in Lutsk didn't cost just three dollars only because it was Eastern Europe. It cost only three dollars because, following the Russian invasion in 2014, Ukrainian currency suffered catastrophic devaluation. The hryvnia had since stabilized but never returned to its pre-invasion levels. Before the Russian invasion, a dollar had bought eight hryvnias. It now bought twenty-five. If I'd visited this restaurant in 2013, the carbonara would have cost about ten dollars—which was still cheap but not cheap enough to make me wonder how the business could possibly pay its employees.

We ordered pizzas, waters, and a latte for Oksana.

"Tell me please, how do you like Ukraine?" Oksana said.

"I like it very much. People are very nice here."

"They are?"

"Maybe 'nice' isn't the right word."

"You use 'nice' quite a lot."

"It's the American in me," I said with a nervous laugh. I was waiting for the blow of the reprimand for my outburst at Serhii. I didn't think that Oksana had any authority over me, but neither did I have any authority over Serhii, and besides all that, I had acted like an asshole and had no defense. If she wanted to do it now, that was fine, and if she wanted to do it the American way and small-talk first, that was fine, too.

"I should rephrase. Ukrainians are not 'nice' like Americans are. We'll smile and give you directions or recommendations on where to eat—things to make you feel welcome. We're friendly. But, as we like to say, friendliness is kindness without any follow-through." I wasn't sure why I presented a thought that had just popped into my head as if it were an American expression. "If you want an American to do anything that inconveniences them or requires real effort, they are among the least likely people to do it. Ukrainians are different, I think. In my brief experience, I have not found Ukrainians to be nice. They don't smile at you or say hello. They don't make small talk."

"Yes, this is a very difficult concept for Ukrainians."

"And a lot of that may just be because I'm so bad at Ukrainian."

"Maybe, yes, but also, it's just how we are."

"But I have found Ukrainians to be kind. And patient. When

Ukrainians wait in line, it looks like they're just waiting. When Americans wait in line, we try to make the line go faster."

Oksana nodded. "This is a big difference."

"Do you think that's a leftover from Soviet times—the patience?"

"It's not impossible. During Soviet times, there was a lot of waiting. Waiting in line for everything." She paused. "There's a joke that older people, my parents' age, if they see someone waiting, anywhere, they'll just get in line behind them, without even asking what they're waiting for."

I wondered if that was a real joke or if Oksana was framing her thoughts as established parts of Ukrainian culture.

The waitress brought out Oksana's latte and our waters. She twisted off the caps to the glass bottles and poured them into glasses. The water was room temperature. I hadn't yet drunk any cold water in Ukraine.

"I am somewhat acquainted with American culture," Oksana said. She related that she'd lived in America on exchange when she was young and had also recently taken a series of online pedagogy courses from an American university. I was surprised, given how un-American her pedagogy was.

"In America, it is a much more democratic system than here," Oksana said. "The professor talks, and the students talk, and it's a collaboration. Maybe you bring a sandwich to eat in class, maybe some coffee. It's relaxed. It's a conversation. In Ukraine, it's formal. The professor thinks he is the king. He should talk, and the students should listen." She took a sip of her latte through a straw; I wondered if that was a Ukraine thing or an Oksana thing. "To my mind, I prefer the democratic system. But frankly speaking, Ukrainians are not ready for it."

I thought it sounded like something a dictator would say to explain why he gassed protesters. I suspected that it was just Oksana who favored the older pedagogy—but it would be harder for me to argue if it was all Ukrainians.

"But how do you know they're not ready for it if you don't try?"

"I have tried. But you cannot learn one way your whole life and then one sunny day say, okay, now we're going to do it a different way. It's too difficult for the students." She paused. "But I try to find balance. You make the solution to fit the situation. All people are good."

I couldn't follow how she'd gotten to her conclusion, but nevertheless, I saw an opportunity. "I appreciate that. But we have to teach the agents to sound American. Given the situation, wouldn't it make sense to use an American solution?"

"Only if it works," she said. Before I could respond, she began to speak again. "When I was a young girl, you couldn't just go into the store and buy clothes—you had to wait for the soldiers to bring them. When the soldiers came, everyone would queue up to get the clothes, and when you got to the front of the queue, you would take what you could. You couldn't worry about size or style."

The waitress brought over two thin-crust pizzas covered in sausages and salamis, the meat baked deep into the cheese and the crust risen into a slightly browned crunch.

"Once, the soldiers came with the clothes and we queued up to wait like we always did. But on this day, instead of handing out the clothes, the soldiers took the clothes to a field and set them on fire."

I waited for Oksana to explain the point, but instead she began cutting her pizza.

"Why did they do that?" I finally said.

She shrugged. "Why did they do anything?"

Before I could try to pull a moral from the story, she said, "John, I have a favor to ask."

I braced myself. I would have to apologize to Serhii, to her, to everyone, probably. I was planning on apologizing to Serhii anyway—but it was so embarrassing to be asked to do it.

"My students at the university, many have never spoken with a native speaker."

I waited. "You want me to speak to your class?"

"Yes."

I exhaled. "Sure. No problem."

"You may speak about whatever you like. It's not so important what you say. It will just be useful to hear you speak."

"I'd be happy to," I said. It was strange to be asked to speak not for the content of what I said but so that the audience could analyze how I was saying it—felt less like being a guest speaker and more like a test subject—but I was mostly just happy there'd been no confrontation.

Oksana drove us back to the office. I shook all the developers' hands in wordless greeting, as was customary, and when I got to Serhii I said, "Sorry about yesterday." He seemed confused but shook my hand, said "*Dobre*," and everyone seemed to treat me normally again. I wasn't sure if Oksana had made some signal that things were okay now or if everyone had just forgiven me—or if it hadn't been a big deal to begin with and I'd just made it so in my head.

I WOULD NOT HAVE AGREED TO GO BOXING WITH DIMA HAD HE asked me on any other day. But he asked on a Friday when I was feeling particularly good about myself. I'd just heard back from Davey on my first progress report. It wasn't exactly best practices for me to be the one scoring the agents, but Davey's technical officer hadn't sorted out the snags in the customer satisfaction surveys yet, and without customer feedback, evaluation fell on me. I tried to be unbiased, but it was clear to me that after our five weeks together the agents were already showing improvement. I reported an average one-point increase in *attentive listening*, *respectful tone*, and *small talk*, and two-point increase in *American diction* and *questions rather than commands*. Davey responded to my fifteen-hundred-word email with: *This is great Turner better than I even expected, keep it up.* I didn't care about the brevity, since the quality of a person's emails was inversely proportional to their power. I even forgot that I didn't really respect Davey's opinion and focused on the fact that he had created this office and all its jobs. It felt good that he approved of my work. So when Dima asked if I wanted to go boxing the next day, I thought, *Why not!* I was the kind of person who could just go boxing in Ukraine and not feel intimidated.

After a night full of regret, I met Dima at the fountain in front of the park near my apartment. I was scared of boxing but more scared of canceling and risking offending Dima, since I didn't know the polite way to get out of things in Ukraine. Dima was in great spirits and drove us in his car—one of those golf-ball-looking European models that don't exist in the United States—to a sports complex on the outskirts of town. From the outside, it looked like a big suburban mall. When Dima had described the complex, I had assumed there were some language barriers at work, as he had said it was a great place for cinema, football, and art. But as it turned out, the only barrier had been to my frame of reference. Inside the mall-looking structure, among other amusements, there was a movie theater, an indoor soccer field, and a modern art museum.

"Tell me, John, do you know Lomachenko?" Dima said.

I had, since moving to Lutsk, learned that the Ukrainian boxer Vasyl Lomachenko was the current lightweight champion of the world. "Of course," I said, trying to hide the nerves in my voice.

"He used to train here."

"Really?"

"No." Dima laughed, and I laughed along.

He led me upstairs toward the sound of thudding and yelling. We entered a musty room where ancient floor fans were spinning at full speed. I was incredibly uncomfortable and very much regretting this decision. I knew, without looking at anyone, that they were all looking at me, and that they would soon be laughing at me, either quietly or aloud. I tried to ground myself, focus on the objects in the room instead of my thoughts. Six heavy punching bags hung from one wall. Two speed bags and a few other contraptions I didn't recognize hung from another. A low, old boxing ring stood in the back. It looked homemade and had the feel of a tree house that might, but probably wouldn't, fall out of the tree. It reminded me of the tiny makeshift stages at youth centers, VA basements, and karate gyms from my high school days where I used to see hardcore and metalcore bands play Friday night shows. I loved the music but always felt like a poser, lurking at the edge of the pit, occasionally jumping in, but never fully committing to the supertight jeans, plugs, and joy in violence of the kids who belonged in the scene. As a teenager, I longed for the violence, but I was also scared of it. Not of pain but of the embarrassment of doing it wrong.

Dima led us over to the weight racks, where he pulled out wraps from his bag.

"You know how to wrap your hands?"

I shook my head.

He took my right hand, pushed my fingers apart, and began wrapping the cloth, looping it over my thumb, running it over his wrist, then my knuckles, then up and through each pair of fingers. Across from us, two teenagers were railing the heavy bags with rattling force, exhaling mightily with each punch. An older man in a tracksuit wearing mitts was calling out orders to a lean, middle-height man in his twenties, moving him around the ring while he ordered various punches. I felt their eyes on me, and on Dima wrapping my hand, and tried to focus on how he was doing it so that I wouldn't have to rely on him to do it again.

The trainer in the tracksuit came over and said something to Dima. Dima said something back. It seemed like they were arguing, but they probably weren't. The trainer looked to be about sixty, with a wide face, white hair, and a big nose that looked bent to the left by force.

"Vitaly says he'll give you basics course for one hundred. Okay?" Dima said.

Four dollars seemed like a more-than-fair price.

"Vitaly does not speak English," Dima explained. "Okay, I'll go train now."

"*Ya trokhy rozomiyu ukrainsku,*" I said, trying to keep my breathing steady. "*Ale ne duzhe dobre.*"

"*Deutsch?*" Vitaly said.

"*Ein wenig. Aber nicht sehr gut.*" It was only after finishing the sentence that I realized I had said the exact same thing, in German, about German, that I had said in Ukrainian, about Ukrainian. Since I'd started traveling, most of my time practicing languages had been spent on getting the phrase "I speak a little *X*, but not very well," to sound good enough to make listeners think I was being modest.

Vitaly stood next to me and showed me how to position my feet. He extended his left hand straight out in a jab.

"*Ein*," he said.

I mimicked his motion. Vitaly corrected my wrist so that it locked.

"*Zwei.*" Vitaly threw what I had always thought of as just a punch, cocking his right hand into a fist and thrusting it straight across his body into an imagined opponent's face. Apparently, this punch was called a two.

"*Ni, ni, ni*," he said when I tried. He pointed to his foot, then pivoted on his back toe as he delivered the punch to push the force from his hips into his fist. He guided me through the steps several times until I got it right. Then he went over the motions for four more punches.

Once he was satisfied that I understood the six punches, he put on the mitts. "*Ein!*" he yelled, and held up his left hand. I threw a jab into his mitt. "*Nein!*" he yelled. He hit his left hand hard with his right, demonstrating the force he wanted me to hit with. "*Ein!*" I threw the jab harder this time. "*Zwei!*" I threw a right-hand punch. "*Drei!*" The left hook. "*Atme!*" he yelled. He'd retracted the mitts facedown into his chest, so it wasn't a punch he was asking for. I tried to remember what *atme* meant in German—it wasn't a number. "*Atme!*" he said again. Vitaly exhaled exaggeratedly. *Breathe.* I started exhaling after every punch.

After I threw the uppercuts and the right hook, finishing up the six punches, Vitaly hit me on the side of the head. "Duck!" he yelled, which was either the same word in German as in English or was just the one English word Vitaly knew.

I tried to duck, three times, but each time I either got hit in the head or lost my balance. Vitaly shook his head. He showed me that I was not to duck straight down or lean back, but rather to shift my weight from my front leg to my back leg, so that I rolled under the punch. We tried it again, from the top. I could feel the blood pulsing through me with each punch and each exhalation—it was exhausting!—but the feel of doing it right, of hearing the gloves hit the mitts, had my whole body humming. It was exhilarating! When Vitaly threw the punch at the right side of my head again, I rolled under it perfectly. Then he hit me on the left side of the head.

"Duck!" he yelled.

"Did you like it?" Dima said nearly an hour later, as we left the gym.

"I loved it," I said. It was the truth. My shirt and hair were drenched; I felt delightfully worn out. Nobody was looking at me anymore. The whole time I'd been boxing I hadn't had time to think of anything but the boxing. "Thank you for bringing me."

"You're welcome." Dima looked pleased. "Now maybe we'll see the art?"

The art museum, located between the bumper cars and the handball courts, had a surprisingly well-curated collection of contemporary Ukrainian painting, photography, and installations. I stopped at a large square canvas covered in abstract blocks of primary colors.

"What do you think it means?" Dima said.

"I don't know. Maybe nothing?"

"I have never thought of it this way. I like this."

We lingered at a photograph of about a dozen naked people seated around a table, with medieval platters of meat and goblets of wine before them. They were wearing bear heads over their human heads and holding automatic weapons.

"I think this one means something," Dima said. "It's a symbol."

"Of Russia?" Bears, I had come to understand, had some symbolic connection to Russia.

"Maybe. Yes, I think so." He paused. "Would you like to hear a joke?"

It took Dima a while to get through the joke, as it involved a lot of words that you didn't need for everyday English conversations. But, basically:

When God created Eastern Europe, he carved from the earth three hulking nations: a dull gray valley called Germany, an endless white tundra called Russia, and, between the two, a bursting field of yellow flowers. Ukraine.

When the Ukrainian people saw their new home, they said, "This is impossible." They could not believe their good fortune. They spent days walking the endless fields of yellow flowers, marveling at the richness of the soil, breathing in the crisp air of the Carpathian Mountains, staring in awe at the glimmering Black Sea. They looked to the dull German fields to the west and the barren Russian plains to the east, and then back at the Eden in which they were going to get to spend their lives. They said to God, "What have we done to deserve such bounty? What have we done to deserve such good fortune? Why have you blessed us with such riches?"

And God said to the Ukrainians, "Let me introduce you to the neighbors."

I laughed.

We strolled through the art in happy, tired silence.

Dima dropped me off at the fountain, and as I walked home I struggled to remember the last time I'd made a friend. It was nice—to have spent such an enjoyable afternoon that would make the rest of the weekend alone more enjoyable, too. But when I turned the corner into the courtyard, I saw Natalie. Dressed in a white denim jacket and light blue jeans with white sneakers, she was walking toward me and looking down at her phone.

"Natalie," I said. But she didn't look up from her phone.

When she got closer, I tried again. "Natalie."

She startled, recognized me, and quickly composed herself. "Hello, John."

"I'm sorry. I didn't mean to startle you. I called your name, but you didn't hear me."

"Natalie is not actually my name."

"Of course. I'm sorry. What is your real name?"

"Natalia."

I laughed. "That's very creative."

"Yes, thank you."

"Is Andy's real name just Andriy?"

"No. Andy's name is Sviatoslav."

"Because Sviatoslav is Ukrainian for Andy."

"Of course."

"So why Natalie, then?"

"I don't know." She shrugged. "I like my name."

"You can go by Natalia at work if you like. It's an easy enough name for Americans."

"It's better to have separation." She looked at my sweaty clothes. "You have been doing athletics."

"I was boxing with Dima."

"Tell me, if you hit him, does he stop talking?"

"I don't know. I'll have to get better to find out." I asked if she lived in the area, then worried that it was an inappropriate question. I'd seen a Korean film in which it was suggested that a lady should not tell a man where she lived.

"Nearby. I was going for a small walk."

"Practicing for work?"

"No, it's not a euphemism. I'm actually taking a small walk." She pointed to the park. "Would you like to join? If you are not too tired from listening to Dima talk."

"That sounds great. Let me just go upstairs and change first."

"It's only a small walk. Your clothes are fine."

"Okay. Does your husband want to join us?" I said, hoping she would say no but thinking it would be inappropriate not to ask.

"Anatoly does not speak English."

We strolled back to the fountain, down the stairs, and onto the tree-shaded gravel pathway that cut through the center of the park to the river. We passed a grandmother walking hand in hand with her young grandson, leaning down to ask him questions, looking almost unbearably happy; families enjoying a Saturday afternoon at the playground; vendors selling ice cream; old men smoking on benches, taking in the last hours of unexpected sunshine before winter. It looked like it could have been a park anywhere. But then we turned onto a side path and the grass was overgrown and sprouting rusted carnival rides: a Viking ship, a very small roller coaster, and a Ferris wheel, all painted the Easter yellows and blues they use on brutalist balconies to offset the concrete. It was an experience I'd had many times since coming to Ukraine: for a block or two you feel like you're in Europe, and then all of a sudden you're in the Soviet Union.

I related the day's boxing lesson, turning the exhilaration I felt—

which was narratively boring—into self-deprecation: the story of getting hit in the head in multiple languages. Natalia smiled without quite laughing. We came upon a couple of strays coming out of the woods: a fluffy white dog and a dog with a black-and-beige coat. They sniffed around us, and though I tried to look unbothered, I couldn't help but tense up.

"I'm still getting used to all the stray dogs," I said after they left.

"They don't have dogs in America?"

"We have lots of dogs, but they have owners. Stray dogs in America aren't friendly like they are here. They're considered dangerous."

"Maybe they are dangerous because they are used to people trying to catch them. Or is that just something from films?"

"No, you might be on to something there," I said. "Who feeds these dogs? They look so well-fed."

"Here, in the center, there are many restaurants that give them old food. The grannies from the apartments give them fish. Outside the city, they are hungrier, and there are men who kill them. But here they have a good life."

"The first week I was here," I said, "I went for a jog in the park. It was dark, there was hardly anyone out, and I had my hood on, my headphones in, and I was right over here when I heard barking. I stopped my music. I turned around and saw two dogs chasing after me. So I took off. I quickly realized that they were faster than me. But I was bigger. So I turned around, put my hands up high, and yelled in my deepest voice, '*Ne! Ne! Ne!*'"

Natalia laughed, the first time I had really seen her laugh. She covered her mouth and shook her shoulders. "Why did you say, '*Ne! Ne! Ne!*'?" she said, happily gasping.

"I figured if I said it in their language, they were more likely to listen."

"And did they?"

"Of course. They stared at me, and then they walked away."

"You understand that you yelled, 'Not! Not! Not!' at them, yes?"

"I thought I was yelling, 'No.'"

"'No' is *ni*. 'Not' is *ne*."

"Whatever I said, it did the trick. They probably thought, *This guy's crazy. Let's get out of here.*"

"I'm impressed, John. You scared them away with your bad Ukrainian."

"I'm very talented."

We walked down to the river, a narrow body of water carbonated with bugs, with the same few feet separating us as before—only now I felt like she was closer. The grass around the waterfront was full of people picnicking in the good weather. On the other side of the river was farmland—flat fields and barns and cows. The sun gave off a soft warmth that had dried my clothes. A light breeze drifted over from the fields. I felt greedy for more of this moment.

We came upon a row of stands selling beer, ice cream, coffee, and barbecued pork on skewers. I asked if Natalia wanted a coffee, since a beer felt too intimate. She ordered a latte, and I ordered an Americano and insisted on covering the whole $1.50 tab, to some annoyance from Natalia. We sat down at a rickety metal table. I asked what she thought about the Ukrainian presidential election coming up next year.

"Why do you want to know about this?"

"Because I live here. I feel like I should know about the politics."

"Pol*it*ics," she said, emphasizing the second syllable of the word instead of the first, "are boring."

"Maybe. But this is only the second election since the revolution, right? Isn't that important?"

"Yes and no. After Maidan, there was a lot of hope. Maybe it made people care about politics more. Now, not so much."

"Do you think it will be Poroshenko again? Or Tymoshenko? Or someone new?"

She shrugged. "You are more interested in Ukrainian politics than most of my friends—and they are actually Ukrainian. Maybe it's because you're used to having good presidents."

"Hardly."

"But you've had some. Maybe Trump is bad, okay, maybe Obama is bad. I don't know. But Lincoln was good, yes?"

"He did free the slaves."

"Yes, you see, Ukrainians are still slaves. We haven't had our Lincoln."

I felt the urge to point out that even if Ukrainians were trapped in a corrupt economic system and even if they had suffered a century of Russian colonial abuse, they were not slaves like the ones Lincoln freed. But I also didn't want to stop Natalia from telling me whatever she was going to tell me.

"Our first president after the end of Soviet Union, in the hard nineties, he ruined everything. During this time, if you were not a criminal, everything was difficult and dangerous. Money became worthless. Then, our next president, he stole everything. We had him for ten years. He tried to kill his enemies, attacked journalists." She sipped her latte through her straw. "His helper, Yanukovych, was to be the next president. Another butler for Russia. But then there came a politician who was not for Putin, who was for the West, and the people liked him. So he was poisoned. But he did not die. So instead they stole the election from him. But this time, we said no. That was when we had to have our first revolution. Two thousand four. The Orange Revolution. Yanukovych was thrown out and we elected our own president."

She paused. "But the president we picked was very disappointing.

He survived the poisoning admirably. But once he was elected, he just talked and did nothing. Nothing changed. He was so bad that for the next election, we elected Yanukovych without him even cheating. We had a revolution to get this man out—and then we voted him back fairly. After that, Yanukovych knew he could not be stopped. He ended up being the worst of all."

I had read about the infamous Yanukovych. Deeply in Putin's pocket, he imprisoned his political opponents, smuggled tens of billions in state funds to his cronies and international accounts, and generally behaved like a dictator. He kept a Saddam Hussein–style pleasure palace, equipped with priceless furniture and a full-size zoo, while much of the country struggled to survive.

"When Yanukovych was president," Natalia continued, "nobody could start a business. Unless you were his son, of course. If you were a son of the president, this was a great time. But no foreign investors wanted to come to Ukraine, because any sunny day a man could just walk up to you and say, 'I'll buy your business, this is how much I'm going to pay for it.' And you can't say no.

"So in 2013 and 2014, we had to have another revolution. Maidan. This one was much more violent. Many died. But it was successful. Yanukovych was forced out and fled to Russia. The next president, the one we brought in with Maidan, was Poroshenko, who, as you know, is running for reelection now."

She sighed. "Poroshenko does some things well. Now you can start a business without fear that it will be stolen. That's important. You can travel to Europe without a visa, which is very important. We're closer to the EU than we've ever been, but they still won't let us join. There's more stability in Ukraine now. And he's only been president for four years. In four years, I can't fix everything in my apartment—how is he supposed to fix everything in a country like Ukraine?"

She paused. "But it's not enough. He is not doing enough. In the winter, most people pay half their salary for heating expenses. My husband's grandparents, during the winter, their whole pension—one hundred Euros per month—goes to paying for gas so they do not freeze."

"Why is heat so expensive?" Despite having less than 10 percent of the income of Americans, by my calculations Ukrainians paid about the same price at the pump—and apparently on their gas bills—as Americans.

She shrugged. "Because they steal."

"Who?"

"Everyone. All the politicians. We can't buy gas from Russia anymore since Maidan, so it's more expensive. Except we have our own gas here in Ukraine. But we have to buy it from the gas company like it's imported."

Maxim had tried to explain this problem to me at the office—the excessive price of gas despite the fact that Ukraine had a supply of natural gas—but he might as well have tried to teach me about subprime mortgages in a second language.

"What do you think is better: Another five years of Poroshenko? Or somebody new?"

She shrugged. "I don't know. Ukraine will not change in five years. Maybe in fifty years. Maybe it's good to have someone new. But frankly speaking, they are all thieves."

I had read that, even after the revolution and the significant reforms it had brought, Ukraine was still ranked as the second most corrupt country in Europe, after only Russia, and was tied with Moldova for poorest country in Europe. In the upcoming election, there were already dozens of candidates and parties in the race, but they were hard to tell apart. I had noticed that the American media tended to focus on the supposed rise of the far right in Ukraine, but I couldn't figure out why, since, unlike in Poland and Hungary, or much of Western Europe, where the fascists were thriving, the far-right party had won just over 1 percent in the last Ukrainian election.

A girl in a wedding dress and a young man in a tuxedo walked by our table holding hands, trailed by a photographer. They looked to be about twenty.

"Are people this young when they marry in America?" Natalia said.

"Not where I'm from. But it depends a little on where you live. Most of my friends are just getting married now, in their early thirties."

"This is why you left? No friends to go to the pub with anymore?"

I smiled. "How old were you when you married?"

"Twenty-one."

"Is that early for here?"

"In Lutsk? Maybe average. Here, you know, for most people, work's not so good, school's not so good—many people want a place where they can be important. So they start a family early."

"But you didn't start a family. You only married."

She shrugged. "Maybe I feel important at work."

After we finished our coffees, I walked Natalia home, to a five-story concrete apartment building near the elementary school, a few blocks from my place.

We faced each other in front of the steps to the front door. I didn't know the appropriate way to part—with a handshake or a hug—but she settled it by waving and saying, "Goodbye, John."

"Goodbye, Natalia."

When I got home, I took a shower and found, happily, that it was my body, rather than my mind, that was very tired. I lay down for a nap and hovered in shallow, unharsh sleep that was kind of like a hand stroking my hair. When I woke it was dark out, but I didn't feel frightened or disoriented. I opened a beer from the fridge and looked out the window. The dim outline of the castle in the night. The trees shedding their leaves. The crows tending to their nests. The neighbor's clothesline stale with shirts. The Lvivsky beer cooling my hand—a half-liter bottle from the store for thirty cents. Boxing with Dima. Walking with Natalia. When had my life ever felt so full of purpose? I was providing a valuable tool—knowledge of how to speak English like an American—that could help lift people out of poverty. I was liked. I was wealthy. I was content. I had been going about things all wrong. Life wasn't about achievement. It wasn't about becoming a great journalist. It was about being useful. Finding a place to belong. I didn't need America. I didn't need sex. I didn't need journalism. I had everything I needed here.

I took a breath and tried to memorize this happiness. I had been so unfair to myself for so long, memorizing only moments of pain. I could recall exactly how my jeans had felt against my leg when Gene had called about my dad. *There's no good way to say this.* The itchy dryness of air-dried jeans. The way Maureen had quietly started crying when I'd said, "This isn't working anymore, is it?" But did I remember what it felt like the first time I kissed Maureen? The first time I published an article? The time we saw the sun set over Tbilisi, from that lookout point Maureen and I just stumbled upon, where stray cats mingled with beer drinkers on benches, and the city stretched out before us half-futuristic and half-ancient in that magical sunset light that only appears on vacation? Well, apparently. But I had to go rummaging around for that memory; it was not the kind of thing my mind played when I was trying to sleep at night. The bad ones were always right there on the surface. No wonder I'd been so unhappy when I spent so much time remembering the wrong things.

It was just as I was trying to record and store away this happy moment here in my apartment that the yelling next door started. My neighbors had been quieter lately—a few raised voices here and there but nothing prolonged. But now the man was yelling again, something about "woman" and "wife." The woman cut him off, yelled something as if she was making a point, stretching out and emphasizing particular words or syllables. The man yelled back. A fist slammed against a table or wall.

Dima had said there was nothing to do. There weren't even police to call about this. But Dima was a man. Maureen said that men were more likely than women to ignore people who might be in danger, because they were less likely to imagine themselves as vulnerable to the same danger. I had to do something. But I didn't know what. Oksana would be the person to ask for advice about this. But calling this late would be inappropriate. Instead, I called Maureen.

She didn't answer.

Why would she? It was a Ukrainian number she didn't recognize.

I texted: *Hey, it's Turner—calling from abroad!*

The woman next door was frantically yelling a stream of something. It sounded like she might be crying.

I called again.

"Turner?"

"Hey, Mo!"

"Hey." She sounded confused. "How are you? How's Ukraine?"

"Oh, you know, it's good. How'd you know I moved to Ukraine?"

"What do you mean? You posted pictures."

"Of course. I was all prepared to explain to you that I'd moved to Ukraine."

"You still can if you want. How is it?"

"Very strange. But I'm enjoying it. My job's interesting."

"Good. That's really good." She paused. "What is your job?"

"I'm teaching call center agents how to interact with Americans. It's actually kind of fascinating."

"Oh." She paused. "That's different. But it sounds like it would be great for you. Congratulations."

"Thanks. How are you?"

"Good, good. You know, things are pretty much the same. No transatlantic moves here."

"Did you get the promotion?"

"Oh yeah, that was a while ago, but I did, actually."

"Congratulations!"

"Thank you. I appreciate that."

I felt a tug at my heart that we weren't dancing in the kitchen—that I wasn't picking her up and singing her name to the tune "Jolene." *Maureen, Maureen, Maureen, Maureeeeeen! I knew that you were gonna get that job!* I wanted to push us back to that place, if only for a few minutes, even if we wouldn't have been happy there for longer than that. But it would have been selfish to try. And there were more pressing matters.

"Hey, I know it's weird me calling you like this. I'm sorry about that. But I need your advice on something and it's a little urgent."

"Okay."

"You were always good about knowing when to intervene."

"Turner. What's going on?"

"My neighbor is hitting his wife."

"Right now?"

"Right now, they're just yelling. But last time they yelled like this, he hit her."

"You need to call the cops."

I explained the situation—how the police here didn't respond to domestic violence calls.

"That complicates things." She thought about it for a minute. "Knock on their door."

"And say what? I don't speak Ukrainian. And they won't speak English."

"You don't have to say anything. Just knock on the door and then leave."

"What do you mean?"

"You knock on the door, hard, like you're a big man—which, by the way, you kind of are—and then you go straight back to your apartment before they answer. You don't have to confront him. Just let him know that you're there."

"Do you think that will help?"

"I don't know. But it's worth a try. If nothing else, it might disrupt the escalation."

"Okay." I took a deep breath. "Good. I'll do that. Thank you. I'm glad I called."

I waited for her to say that she was glad, too, but she didn't. "Be careful. Don't try to fight him or anything stupid. Take care of yourself."

When I put down the phone, my adrenaline was rushing. I opened another beer and drank half of it in one swallow. I put on my shoes. The voices were rising. Then he hit her. She screamed.

I charged into the hallway and pounded on their door. I pounded as hard as I could. I kept knocking and knocking until the meat of my hand was throbbing. I didn't go back to my apartment like Maureen had said. I stood there waiting for a fight. I clenched my fists. In my head I practiced the two-punch Vitaly taught me. The man said something inside. The woman said something insistent through her tears. It sounded like he was coming to the door. But she stopped him. Then it got quieter. I knocked again, softer this time. No sound. I stood there waiting, but no one appeared. I heard the front door to the building open downstairs, then steps coming up the stairs. I hurried back to my apartment.

Inside, I looked for a weapon in case the man changed his mind. I removed a dull but large kitchen knife from the drawer but quickly admitted to myself that I couldn't stab anyone. Instead, I grabbed a broom from the closet and unscrewed the head from the hard plastic rod. I paced around the apartment with the broomstick in my hand, worrying that I'd done the wrong thing. But I suspected I'd done the right thing. Right or wrong, it felt jittery and terrible. I wanted to call Maureen and tell her what I'd done and have her reassure me that this was good. But that would've been selfish.

I listened for hours. It was quiet. Either he had stopped or killed her.

When I opened my eyes in the morning, the adrenaline jolted me straight awake. I bolted up. There was no sound from next door. It was 7:30. I'd been asleep for maybe three hours. But there was no hope of going back to sleep. I took a shower and dressed to go to the market. I would pick up a baguette, a salami, a carton of juice, and a bag of the one imported coffee they carried. Maybe I could walk off some of this energy—shake off some of the shakes. I had intervened. I had done what I could. So why did I feel so shitty?

I put on my shoes. Put in earbuds and played a basketball podcast. One of the great things about the modern world was that there were always people talking about basketball—a subject that did not matter at all but that I cared about deeply. As faraway voices began to speak into my ears, I opened the front door, stepped into the hallway, and froze. Staring back at me, closing my neighbor's door, about to walk down the stairs, dressed in jeans and a white denim jacket, with a purple bruise over her left eye peeking out from behind her makeup, was Natalia.

"Good morning, John," she said.

"Good morning, Natalia." I was dumb with surprise. "I didn't know you lived here."

She shrugged. "Yes."

I couldn't find the right words. The gentle ones. Caring ones. Appropriate ones. "Are you okay?"

"Yes," she said neutrally. "And how are you today?"

"I'm . . ." I paused. Before I could speak, she cut me off.

"You knocked last night."

"I just wanted to help." I paused. "Do you need help?"

"No."

"Can I do anything?"

"No. It's okay. I fell."

"You fell?"

She shrugged. "It's a euphemism."

I started to speak, but she cut me off again.

"I'll see you at the office, John."

And with that, she left.

JANUARY 2019

It was three days after Orthodox Christmas, the Christmas observed in Ukraine, and I was on my way to my fifth ATM of the day, collecting the money I was going to use to bribe Anatoly. It was an idea I'd had that morning, and once it occurred to me I was amazed that I hadn't thought of it in the months since I discovered who my neighbors were. Since the foreign bank was closed today, presumably for some holiday, I had to hit several ATMs to withdraw the amount I needed.

The streets of Lutsk were snowy and emptier than usual. Martial law had recently ended, but that hadn't affected the number of people on the streets, since the martial law itself hadn't affected the number of people on the streets. It had started in November when Russia illegally seized three Ukrainian boats in the neutral waters between Russian-occupied Crimea and mainland Russia. It had been notable as the first overt act of war on the part of the Russian government, which had been claiming since the beginning of the Russian invasion in 2014 that there was no Russian invasion. By their account, it was simply Russian tourists who had streamed into Crimea and the Donbas region of Eastern Ukraine to fight alongside Ukrainian rebels who wanted to be annexed to Russia. Ukrainians called these tourists "little green men," which I assumed carried some untranslatable subtext, but the point was that they were not tourists but Russian military dressed in unmarked green uniforms. But now the Russian military was openly seizing boats, and in response the Ukrainian government declared martial law. I actually didn't hear about the situation until I read about it in the *New York Times*. Granted, Lutsk was about seven hundred miles west of the war zone in a place where the martial law did not affect our movements or routines, but it was still strange—learning about the place you live from people who aren't there. If not for the internet, I might not have known it was happening at all.

The streets were emptier today because of the holidays. The office had been closed since New Year, the beginning of the Ukrainian holiday season, and would remain closed for another week. Other businesses and schools had more amorphous breaks, and a lot of people were out of town. Oksana told me that the university would be closed for winter break until "it depends," since heating the cavernous school during the coldest months was too expensive. Classes would resume sometime between late February and mid-March, depending on the weather. But the little yellow *marshrutka* buses still zigzagged down Prospekt Voli, the old ladies in headscarves still strode with authority on wobbly legs, and stray dogs in thick winter coats still patrolled the sidewalks, politely searching for food, seeming happy and undesperate even in the fifteen-degree chill.

At the ATM, I withdrew the maximum amount, and as the machine spit out a small stack of yellow 200-hryvnia notes, softened with age, I felt a dizzying sense of purpose. I bent down like I was tying my shoe and stuffed the bills into my sock, surely fooling no one, had anyone been watching. I calculated that between my socks, the inner pockets of my jacket, and the waistband of my underwear, I had about $1,000 in cash—half of what I needed. Two thousand dollars, or 50,000 hryvnias, was an arbitrary amount, but it was the sum I had decided would be too much for Anatoly to refuse. Last night, he'd gone too far with Natalia. He had to be stopped. And I had the means to stop him. It was what a good person would do. I wished that my dad could see me. Then I felt ashamed—that I hadn't been there to stop it in the first place and was only reacting after the fact.

I noticed, as I adjusted my money-filled sock, that my toes were freezing. I stepped into a café to warm up. I ordered an Americano, which was not good but was at least hot. Back outside, the cold bit my face again. Nobody salted the streets here and I had to remind myself to be mindful of each step. Since winter started, I had fallen twice, once bruising my hip and once spraining my wrist. I was still bad at keeping my balance, but I knew to go slower, which eliminated most of the danger. Frustratingly, I seemed to be the only one struggling with the ice. As I carefully planted and grounded each step before lifting my other foot, I saw Ukrainian women briskly moving across the ice in high heels while texting, talking to a friend, and corralling children.

One afternoon, a few weeks earlier, I had asked Natalia, who'd arrived at the office wearing brown leather heels, how Ukrainian women could traverse the ice like that without falling.

"Our secret," she said, whispering conspiratorially, "is that we fall all the time."

By that point, Natalia and I were back to joking and half flirting again. The day after the violence next door, she'd come into the office with her black eye so well hidden under makeup that I might not have noticed if I hadn't known to look. I waited until we had a second alone, then asked her how she was doing.

"So far so good, can't complain, thank you," she said. "And how is your day going, sir?" She'd given a wry smile. I hadn't known how to respond. To tell a joke and be met by pity was terrible. But to have your boss laugh at your trauma wouldn't have been too fun either.

The following day at the office, I'd told her that if she ever wanted to talk, I was around. She acted like she didn't know what I was referring to and then avoided me for the rest of her shift. I felt terrible about doing nothing when she was being abused; also terrible for pushing her into an uncomfortable position when she clearly didn't want to talk about it. The next day I said nothing about the attack, and the day after that I said nothing, and the more days I went without saying anything, the easier it got to say nothing.

Then, after several days of my saying nothing, Dima dropped me off after Saturday boxing, and I'd found Natalia waiting by the fountain.

"Fancy a walk?" she'd said. I didn't laugh since I wasn't sure if the "fancy" was meant to be funny.

We strolled through the park, chilly in the mid-November wind, keeping ourselves warm with a brisk pace, and talked about everything but her home life.

"Are American call centers like ours?" she said as we came down the stairs to the river.

"They're similar," I said, though I'd never been to an American call center. "Most are bigger than ours. And you get paid more."

A little later, she said, "What's Los Angeles like? I've seen it on television, of course, but I wonder how realistic that is."

Her question made me a little dizzy with implication.

"It's a big city. But more than that, it's a wide city. It was built after the car was invented, so instead of building up, we built out. It's sixty kilometers to drive from one end to the other—but that just means there's lots to see. It's warm all year round. There's great food. It's not as expensive as New York and San Francisco. A lot of people there work in the movie industry, but not that many are actors. You do see actors out sometimes, though. One time I saw—"

"But what do *you* think of when you think of Los Angeles?"

She clearly didn't want the chamber of commerce pitch, so I thought about it for a minute and tried to be honest. I said that I thought of blue street signs. Stringbean palm trees. Constant sunshine filtered through a gauzy curtain of smog. Strip malls and 7-Elevens. Billboards and underpasses. I said I thought of how hot winds blew in from the desert at the end of every summer and started fires. How the fires made ash rain from the sky. How my dad and I used to play catch under the ashes and pretend it was snowing. How I had memories of every exit sign on the 101 Freeway, even the exits I'd never taken, because I'd spent so much time sitting in traffic.

"It sounds terrible!" Natalia said with a laugh. "Dirty air, fires, traffic—"

"And palm trees."

"Yes. Those do sound nice."

"I was eighteen when I moved away, and I promised myself I'd never live in LA again. But I do love it. Everything that's terrible about it is also wonderful in the way that only home is."

She nodded. "Now I understand."

"It's also really beautiful. People travel from all over the world to visit. You have beaches and mountains and forests and bustling city centers, all just a few minutes away."

"Frankly speaking, this is much better marketing, John."

I laughed. "Would you like to visit America someday?" I said, trying to make my voice sound as casual as possible.

She shrugged. "We will see. There are many other places to visit first."

When we returned to the fountain, I pretended to have an errand to run to spare her the discomfort of me walking her back to our building. We didn't talk about America again, but the walk became a weekly routine—one that I greatly looked forward to. My life in general had settled into a steady routine: along with my Saturday walks with Natalia and boxing with Dima, there was work, reading, trying to learn Ukrainian, and watching TV. Even if it felt lonely at times, it was comforting to have such a clear schedule of five days of work, one day of socializing, one day of rest. There were no decisions to be made, no mistakes looming. I was serving a purpose, and life was simple. Or it had been simple. But then the holidays came and everything turned complicated.

The morning of American Christmas, which was just a regular day in Ukraine, I was searching through the market for something to cook for dinner. Turkeys weren't available, but there also weren't any hams, as they weren't an item sold in Lutsk. The closest thing to a festive main course I could find was a whole chicken. I grabbed it, along with some potatoes and carrots still dusted in soil, and headed off to the cookie aisle to find some dessert. It was there that I heard the sound of a woman speaking American English. The only other time I'd heard American English in Lutsk had been from the Mormon boys in ties and name tags standing on Vynnychenka. In the beginning, I tried to strike up conversations out of sympathy, since I could imagine few things more difficult than trying to sell a new religion in a place where the vast majority of people were Ukrainian Orthodox, wary of strangers, and didn't speak English. But I stopped attempting small talk once I realized how reluctant they were to turn off their sales pitch. Try to talk about the weather, Ukrainian food, basketball—they'd just bring it back to God.

I assumed the English-speaking voice in the market that day belonged to a missionary as well, but when I turned the corner I saw two women without name tags. One of the women had red hair and wore an unzipped black puffer jacket that went all the way down to her winter boots; the other had blond hair and wore a short peacoat, stockings, and high heels. They looked like an American and a Ukrainian.

"The chocolate ones are good, but let's get some stroopwafels, too," the red-haired American said. "I know they're expensive, but I'll pay for them. It's Christmas, after all."

"Excuse me," I said. "You wouldn't happen to be American, would you?"

"I am." She said something to her companion in rapid Ukrainian that was too fast for me to understand. She looked to the place on my shirt where a name tag would be. "And you're American, too?"

We chatted a little and explained our reasons for being in Ukraine. Muriel was here with Peace Corps and taught English in a nearby village. She was kind of cute, but loud and literal, and we talked for three or four minutes without making each other laugh a single time. But she was American. So when her companion went off to grab something and Muriel asked for my number—rather than asking if I was on Facebook or WhatsApp, which is what a Ukrainian would have done—I gave it to her. And later that day, when she interrupted my solitary Christmas chicken roasting with a text inviting me to a New Year's Eve party, I happily accepted.

The party, I learned when she texted me the address, was on the ground floor of the building where I worked. As it was one of the newer buildings in town, the banquet room downstairs was a favored location for conferences, presentations, viewing parties to watch Lomachenko fights, and salsa dancing nights, which would sometimes be happening when I left work. I'd once attended a salsa night there with Dima, but going out at night when you weren't looking to meet someone and everyone had to struggle through a second language to include you felt like a chore, and I'd left early.

I asked Muriel if I should bring anything.

If you want to, Muriel wrote back unhelpfully.

I bought a bottle of American bourbon for ten dollars from Wine Time, the fancy wine store on Lesya Ukrainka. The same bourbon cost about twenty dollars in Portland, but I didn't understand how things like that worked. Some American imports, like clothes and computer accessories, were more expensive in Ukraine than in America; other imports, like the few food products available—certain brands of chips, alcohol, toothpaste, and soda—were cheaper in Ukraine. Even if the same bottle of mid-shelf bourbon cost ten dollars in Lutsk and twenty dollars in Portland, the average citizen of Lutsk would have to work five hours to buy that bottle while the average citizen of Portland would have to work about one hour to buy the same bottle. As a citizen of Portland currently squatting in Lutsk, I had to work about thirty minutes to earn enough to buy the bottle. I didn't know what to do with that knowledge. The ethical thing would probably have been to start paying Ukrainian taxes. But I had no visa, as Davey had said that I didn't need one—visas, residency permits, and taxes would muddy the whole situation unnecessarily.

"You can come for ninety days with just an American passport," he'd explained, "and if you stay longer than that, it's no big deal." Whenever I decided to leave Ukraine and they saw that I'd overstayed my visa at customs, Davey said that it was only a thirty-dollar fine paid at the airport and no one really cared. "They're just happy to have someone bringing jobs and money to the region. The only people who might get upset are the cops. Just don't get arrested and you can stay for as long as you want." I had since suspected that it probably was a big deal that I was working here without permission and without paying taxes, and that it was just advantageous for Davey to not have me on the books in either country. But it was advantageous for me, too, and interrogating the ethics any further would have involved waiting in line at embassies and tax offices, and probably filling out a lot of forms.

When I walked into the New Year's Eve party, I saw thirty or forty people standing around tall tables. A Russian hip-hop video was playing on a large projector screen. I worried a little bit about whether it was inappropriate to have brought my own liquor. I was also thinking the vain and comforting thought that at least I looked good. In LA, I felt that I was average looking, and in Portland, just slightly-above-average looking. But here, my clothes fit better than those of the other men, I had a stronger hairline, and I was taller and leaner than most. It made me feel confident to walk into a room and be, or at least think I was, one of the most attractive men there—as if I'd done something to earn it.

I saw Muriel at a table near the bar talking to two other girls. She wore a dark green dress that complemented her fair skin and red hair in a soap-commercial kind of way. She was prettier than I had initially thought. She waved me over. Someone handed me a glass of white wine. I put my bottle under the table.

We chatted about her work. Her job at the high school, I learned without asking, paid $275 per month, since Peace Corps volunteers were paid the average local salary. She had some good students, she said, but the boys were terrible.

I told her that it sounded like America.

She responded that it was not like America.

"No, of course not. I just meant in America, the shitty students are usually boys, too."

"Not like these."

Even over the loud music, it was noticeable how loud a talker she was, but luckily it didn't seem to draw attention the way it had in the grocery store. We drank more. She talked about the host family she lived with—how the father was fine until he got drunk and then would reach out and grab her if there was no one else around. She would have to shut herself in her room with a doorstopper she'd asked her sister to mail from home.

I asked her if she'd ever thought of leaving.

"I used to think about it every day. But I've been here for sixteen months, so I'm more than halfway through. And leaving at this point would feel like giving up. I really do like most of the students—I don't want to leave them. I think it's just the living situation that's clouding everything."

"John!" said a voice.

I turned to see Serhii, the developer I'd threatened to fire, with two tall, slightly potbellied Ukrainian men with shaved heads.

"Serhii! Happy New Year!" I said, and shook his hand. I looked for signs of resentment but found none. I shook hands with the two other men in silence, as was customary. They did not shake hands with Muriel, since she was a woman, which was also customary. The practice had made me uncomfortable, initially, but I'd grown used to it. But having Muriel, another American, watching me made it uncomfortable again.

"This is my friend Muriel," I said. "She's also American."

"Hello," Serhii said with a wave.

"Hi," said Muriel, a little coldly, I thought. "I'm going to freshen my drink."

"John, please," Serhii said, motioning me into their little circle.

"Whisky," said one of the tall men. He held up a bottle of Johnnie Walker and handed me a glass. "Yes?"

"Please."

The man poured out four whiskies and Serhii said, in English, "Health!"

Our conversation was limited by language, but I complimented the whisky and was handed the bottle.

"Oh, this is a good one," I said. "From Scotland." Everyone nodded in agreement. When we finished the first glass, I went and grabbed my bourbon, showed it to the group, said, "From America," and filled everyone's cup. They nodded their approval and passed the bottle around to inspect. We managed four drinks this way.

When I returned to Muriel, it was closer to midnight and I was much happier. A song was playing by a Russian artist called Matrang that I'd heard a lot during my first month in the country. Despite a cheesy dance beat and overly sincere delivery, I caught myself getting lost in the minor chord progression. A few Ukrainian women were dancing with one another. Then a hip-hop song that was popular when I was in high school came on, and I suggested to Muriel that we dance. It was absurd, but I had enough of a buzz to forget that and enjoy myself. I imagined Natalia there, watching us, making fun of me, which made the dancing even more fun.

When we returned to our table, slightly out of breath, I pointed at the tissue box on the table and said, "Why are these on every table in this country?"

"I know!" Muriel said. "It took months to get used to it. I'm at a restaurant, but I can't get a napkin—I'm supposed to wipe my hands with a tissue."

"Right? And here's a question: everywhere I go, there's a cleaning lady cleaning the floor, all the time."

"Yes!"

"But I've never seen a place with such dirty buildings. Like, what's the point of having such a clean floor if the outside of your building is covered in dirt?"

"Exactly! Oh my god. And how about how no one can say 'yes' just one time? Like, it can't just be *tak*. It has to be *tak tak tak, da da da, dobre dobre dobre, kharasho kharasho kharasho*."

"They actually have to switch to Russian, then back to Ukrainian, then back to Russian again, just to be able to say 'yes' enough times!"

Muriel was shaking from laughter; she was pretty now. I looked over her shoulder at one of the Ukrainian girls who was staring at us. But the music was loud; I thought she probably couldn't hear us. And even if she could—after four months of trying to be polite and considerate, it was a relief not to care for a minute.

"Do they kiss at midnight here?" Muriel said.

"I don't know. You're the expert."

She leaned over and kissed me, then pulled away and smiled, and it was nice—how it happened and then stopped happening, without any action required of me. It was easy to get so wrapped up in the comfort of being alone that you forget how terrible it is to be alone.

When she texted me the next morning to say that she'd had a good time, I wrote back that I had as well, but left it at that. I wasn't against something happening, but I didn't want to set it in motion.

I spent New Year's Day combating my hangover with a walk alongside the frozen waterways of the park. The hangover increased my regret at making jokes about Ukraine at a Ukrainian party, even though I didn't think any Ukrainians had heard me. But maybe they had. Even if they hadn't, it still felt like a shitty thing to do. The memory of those few minutes of acting like a dumb, loud American plastered over the whole rest of the party. I was happy that I hadn't gone home with Muriel. If we'd had sex, I might have totally lost myself in the moment with her. I might have said or done something even worse than making fun of the Ukrainians. And then the shame I was feeling now would be even worse.

I pulled out my phone and texted Natalia.

Happy New Year! I'm in the park. Are you in the mood for a walk?

A minute later my phone plinged. *Certainly)*

Why Ukrainians only used the mouth, and not the eyes, to make a smiley face was a mystery to me. But you could just as well ask why Americans chose to exclude the nose.

We met by the fountain thirty minutes later. I asked her where Anatoly was, and she said, "He is reckoning with the ghosts of yesterday's drinking."

I laughed. "I can sympathize."

"Did it sound stupid the way I said that?"

"No. It was funny."

"Good. I practiced it before I left."

I felt a little hiccup in my chest. "You should be a poet."

"Ukraine has too many poets."

"Lesya Ukrainka," I said, pointing at one of the many statues around town of the nineteenth-century poet and Lutsk's most famous daughter. "And Taras Shevchenko, of course."

"Did you know that all the Shevchenko statues were built after the end of the Soviet Union? They had to replace all the Lenin statues with someone new, so they said, okay, maybe Shevchenko. And now we have so many fucking Shevchenko statues!"

I did know that—it was a detail a lot of travel bloggers liked to include about Ukraine—but I laughed along anyway because it was the first time I'd heard Natalia swear. "I never expected such vulgarity from you."

She was quiet for a beat. "I don't understand."

"I was teasing you. You said 'fucking' and you don't usually say 'fuck,' so I was pretending to be offended, and I was using overly formal language, because I wanted to play off of earlier when you'd said that your husband was reckoning with the ghosts of last night."

"I understand." She paused. "This was a very fucking complicated joke, John."

I started laughing.

"You may not know this, John, but I am not a native English speaker."

I laughed harder, and she kept going, feeling the power of her riff.

"And you may not know this, but I am also reckoning with the ghost of last night. That fucking ghost drank three glasses of cognac after the champagne!"

"Stop!" I said, gasping. "Stop, you're killing me."

When we caught our breath and Natalia wiped a tear from her eye, she asked me what I'd done to celebrate.

"I went to a party with some other Americans. Serhii was there, too."

"Yes, he told me you were at the party."

I'd begun to notice that everyone in the office knew about everything I did before I told them. If I was shopping at the big mall, Tam Tam, they knew about it. If I was jogging in the park, they knew about it. If I left a big tip at the Italian restaurant, they knew about it. I wasn't sure how. Did they have a WhatsApp group where they reported John sightings?

"Serhii said you were with a girlfriend."

I tried to contain a smile. "Not a girlfriend. But a girl, yes."

"And you are in love with her?"

"I am not at all in love with her. It's only the second time I've seen her."

"Okay, maybe the wrong expression. But you have a crush, maybe?"

"No, I don't think so."

"Why not? Serhii said she was pretty."

"I don't know. She's nice. She's American, so we have that in common. But she's very serious. And she talks really loudly. It bothers me."

"This is not a nice way to talk about a girl you love," Natalia said.

"You need to stop."

"Okay, okay," she said, putting her arms up in mock defeat. "I see the love has made you sensitive."

Her eyes were laughing. For a moment, I wished that she and I were married—that we'd been married for a long time, to the point where it was just comfortable and calm. But I pushed that aside.

"But you will see her again?"

"I don't know. I haven't decided."

"What is there to decide? You met a girl. She is pretty. You think maybe you like her. You should see her again."

I was a little disappointed that Natalia wanted me to see Muriel again, as it made me remember who I actually wanted to go out with. But when Muriel texted me, I agreed that it would be fun to hang out again. I suggested Bar 11 on Prospekt Voli or the new cocktail place on Lesya Ukrainka, but Muriel said that it was such a hassle to get to the city from her village and get back at night that we might as well make a day of it.

How about an overnighter in Lviv?

It would have seemed bold in an American context. But a Ukrainian context was a much fuzzier thing—at least in my eyes. I'd been wanting to go to Lviv, anyway, and I had found the prospect of traveling alone much less appealing when I already lived alone. So I told her that sounded good and started looking up Airbnbs.

Two days later, I met her in the waiting room of the Lutsk bus station, an utterly depressing place that looked more like American stereotypes of the Soviet Union than any place I'd visited. Stiff-backed wooden benches, flickering fluorescent lights, and children begging for coins. The bus station wasn't that far from the city center, but even just a few miles outside downtown things got bleak. Muriel was standing near the door. She had her hair tied back and a thick scarf around her neck. We hugged hello and went to the ticket window, where she asked in Ukrainian for two bus tickets to Lviv, about a three-hour ride, and I paid for both, for a total of ten dollars, motioning Muriel's hand away when she pretended to reach for her wallet.

The bus was old and small with a faded picture of a lion painted on the side. It had eighteen seats—including two in the front seat next to the driver—and old curtains that could be pulled over the windows. As we jerked into motion and headed south, Muriel told me about the difficulties of teaching Sylvia Plath to Ukrainian high school students—an experiment she'd recently tried and would not be trying again.

"At the time that Plath was writing, most of my students' grandmothers were working in factories, then coming home to do all the housework. This was the Soviet idea of equality: both genders work grueling hours in factories, but then the women do all the work at home. I had thought that Plath would be universal—or that at least the girls would be able to relate to her. But even they weren't at all sympathetic to the sadness of a privileged American housewife."

As the bus puttered along over potholes and bumps, I learned that Muriel had lots of thoughts about her time in Ukraine just locked up, waiting for the right audience, and with a little encouragement was happy to share them all. I wasn't just being polite either: she knew a lot and listening to her was like taking a guided tour of the country specifically curated to an American my age.

She spoke with disdain of American sexpats who thought it was still the nineties, when a good-looking Ukrainian woman might be compelled to run off with the first foreigner who could get her out. These men didn't realize that there were opportunities in Ukraine now, that it was becoming a place worth staying, and that a ticket to the American middle class wasn't as valuable anymore.

"Now that Ukraine's not tied to Russia, all this IMF, American, and EU money is rolling in. In just a few years, Ukraine has gone from being extremely corrupt and dependent on Russia to about half as corrupt and dependent on the US."

It bothered me how loudly she was talking—loud enough to make the other passengers stare. But she was also teaching me lots of things I didn't know—or at least summarizing the many stand-alone facts I'd read, which had previously failed to stick together into a cohesive narrative.

"But people wondered, even with all this money, who would protect Ukraine if Russia invaded?" she said. "No one, obviously, because the Russians landed in Crimea and the Donbas and neither the US, the EU, nor NATO sent anything more than cash and stern words. But Ukraine survived anyway. What Putin hadn't counted on was that Ukrainians would defend Ukraine."

She took a breath. "There's so much apathy and nihilism here. Generations of brutality have shown that it's better to just accept things the way they are—better to make do than draw attention to yourself. Putin figured he could capitalize on that, along with an admiration for Russia, which is so much richer than Ukraine. He thought Ukrainians, many of whom identify at least partly as Russian, would be happy for a chance at annexation and a Russian passport. He knew he'd never be able to take Kyiv or the Ukrainian-speaking west. But he thought that the Russian-speaking areas in the east and the south—the industrial areas rich in resources—would welcome his little green men. He thought that, tempted by a return to a glorious past that never existed, Russian-speaking Ukrainians would take up arms to fight for Novorossiya." Other passengers turned their heads when she said the word for Putin's manifest destiny catchphrase: "New Russia." I squirmed.

"But the opposite happened. Instead, Ukrainians across the

country—Ukrainian speaking and Russian speaking—risked their lives to fight for Ukraine. In Dnipro, Kharkiv, and Odesa, where Ukrainian nationalism has never been big, the locals fought back the Russians. It was really amazing. The bravery. The selflessness. The putting aside of differences—political, social, economic—to fight for something. And it was something worth fighting for." She paused. "It's easy to forget, because of the poverty and the corruption and just the daily frustration of living here, but this is springtime for Ukraine. Everywhere you look, somebody's building something."

The bus pulled into Lviv in the early afternoon of a frigid and sunny day. Lviv was the biggest city in western Ukraine, with a population of around a million. According to many travel lists, it was one of the hip new places to visit in Eastern Europe, with affordability listed as a big perk. It had been called Lwow, Lemberg, Lvov, and now Lviv, as it moved from Poland, to Austria, to Poland again, then Nazi Germany, then the USSR, and finally Ukraine. But this was the norm for the region. Every time I pulled up a Wikipedia page for an Eastern European writer, their birthplace required a parenthetical explanation. *Born: Stanislav, Ukrainian SSR, Soviet Union (modern Ivano-Frankivsk, Ukraine)*. For countries situated between Germany and Russia, names tended to be temporary.

After dropping off our backpacks at the apartment I'd booked for the night—Muriel reimbursed me for her half of the forty-two dollars, despite my objections—we headed out to explore. We ate varenyky—the traditional Ukrainian dumplings filled with meat and potatoes, topped with sour cream—at a kitschy spot with checkered tablecloths where you could watch old women in headscarves rolling dough through a little window into the kitchen. I thought about how I would describe the place's weird chain-like quality, though I didn't think it was a chain, if I were writing about it. Apparently, the sustained sound of American English had made something in my brain think I was a journalist again.

Muriel talked about how alienated she felt from everything living with her host family out in the country, which, I had to admit, I struggled to pay attention to. She was far less interesting when she was complaining about her personal life than when she talked about Ukraine. It was difficult and time-consuming to get the buses into Lutsk to meet up with the other Peace Corps volunteers in the area, she said. She had joined an online group for Americans teaching English in Europe, but that hadn't helped.

"Most of them are in France or Germany or something and they're dealing with the most First World problems imaginable," she said.

I tried to nod understandingly, but all I could think was: *Why are you talking so loudly?* I couldn't understand how a person so observant and educated about Ukraine didn't notice that she was talking twice as loudly as anyone else in the restaurant. How had she learned so much but not this one basic fact? Ukrainians were only loud when they were drinking. It was currently one in the afternoon in a family restaurant, and here Muriel was yelling about how no one could truly understand how frustrating it was to teach Ukrainians, while a dozen people stared at us.

"Online they're all talking about how difficult it is to get their French students to understand the concept of stating your preferred pronouns, and I'm like, guys, I'm just trying to get my students to stop saying the n-word. I don't understand why, but there is no English word that Ukrainian teenagers like saying more than the n-word."

I braced, hoping she wouldn't actually say it.

"We have like a million words in the English language, but we have to spend all our time on the one word they're not allowed to say. You have no idea how exhausting it is explaining this concept again and again to people who have no conception not only of the English language, but of race relations in general."

"I guess it's hard to explain racism to Ukrainians since it's so white here," I said. She was right that Ukrainian conceptions of race were often outdated at best—to say nothing of homophobia, which was rampant. But I didn't love her tone. "One of the people in my office said that Ukraine doesn't have racism like America because they don't have African Americans. Which is a totally bonkers statement to make. But the fact that they don't understand that it's bonkers shows how far outside their frame of reference the whole issue is."

"But they don't even try!" she yelled. "How hard would it be to just try?"

"I don't know." I felt caught, since the prescriptive importing of culture was imperialist, but anti-racism was anti-imperialist. Not yelling in restaurants had to be anti-imperialist. I ate as quickly as possible in hopes of getting back into the open air.

Outside, it was cold but pretty. Lviv was full of cute streetcars—long, thin, rectangular things that looked like they were from the sixties and probably weren't as cute if you had to take them to work every day. The city felt like a smaller and grittier Vienna, charged with the invigorating feeling that if you found a good spot you might be the only tourist there. There was far more traffic here than in Lutsk and slightly more Western languages to be heard. But it was still overwhelmingly white, overwhelmingly Ukrainian. In the main square, we passed a row of pastel buildings artfully lined up, a photogenic scene that appeared in seemingly every European city square. But here the buildings were a little dirty, because it was Ukraine and who was going to pay for the outside of a building to be cleaned?

I wanted to keep us outside, where Muriel's voice wouldn't be so uncomfortable, but the cold was starting to cut into our bones—it was nine degrees and windy—and after touring the Christmas market I couldn't argue when Muriel insisted that we seek out warmth.

We went to a busy chocolate shop—a tall, narrow building in the center of town, where chocolatiers made chocolate for spectators on the bottom floor, while the three upper floors housed cafés and gift shops. We walked up to the attic café, where the arched ceiling forced me to crouch and every table was filled with rosy-cheeked young people in scarves drinking cocoa from mugs. We ordered cocoa and sat under the slanting ceiling, looking out at the square. The cocoa was rich and sludgy; it tasted delicious and gave me immediate indigestion.

"What's in this?" I said.

"I think it's just chocolate melted down."

"Their slogan should be, 'If you want to drink the best hot chocolate you've ever had, then die from sugar poisoning, come to Lvivsky Chocolate.'"

"They have tea, if you prefer," Muriel answered.

I asked Muriel if she'd ever ridden the streetcars in Lviv, and she said she hadn't.

"I wonder how they compare to the *marshrutkas* in Lutsk," I said.

"I would guess they're about the same."

The Lutsk buses were hot when it was hot outside, and also hot when it was cold outside, as the old ladies never let you open the windows. Apparently, they believed that cold air caused illness. The buses were always crowded and quiet. Passengers passed the money for the fare to the person in front of them, who passed it up the line, until it got to the driver, who had a pile of bills spread out on a blanket on the dashboard and would pull from the pile to pass the change back, no one at all worried about theft.

It was a big contrast from taking public transportation in Portland, where disturbed people frequently yelled at you or tried to imprison you in monologues with no escape. I commented to Muriel that it was strange how, in America, the trains and buses were more comfortable and ran better than in Ukraine but were full of menacing and unstable passengers. In Ukraine, the buses were steamy, miserable, and prone to breakdown. But inside they were calm—there were no disturbances, and everyone followed the rules.

"That's because Ukrainians don't let the mentally ill out of the house," Muriel said.

I wished she would talk quieter when she detailed the faults of Ukrainians.

"It's a source of great shame to have someone in your family suffer from mental illness or even something like cerebral palsy, which has no effect on the brain. But they don't differentiate. To Ukrainians, a defective person is defective. Do you ever see blind people here? Do you ever see people in wheelchairs? It's not because the country takes such good care of them. It's because they're locked away so the rest of the populace won't have to deal with them. That's how you get the buses with no disturbances."

I had, in fact, seen people in wheelchairs in Ukraine. Even if most buildings in Lutsk weren't very accessible, people in wheelchairs certainly weren't "locked up." I wondered how much Muriel really knew about this country.

"I hadn't noticed that," I said.

"It's important to learn about the place you're living," Muriel said, quite confidently for the lone restaurant-yeller in Lviv.

After dinner at a burger spot, I was beat and wanted to go back to the apartment, hoping that maybe some time alone without worrying about the gaze of others would make me attracted to Muriel again. But Muriel had more plans. It was becoming increasingly clear that she'd put together a detailed itinerary for us without consulting me. On the one hand, it made sense, since she had been to Lviv and I hadn't, she spoke Ukrainian and I didn't, and with her planning everything I at least didn't have to worry about bringing her to a place she would find disappointing. But it was still a little grating to be treated like a child.

The next stop was a massive beer hall, where the crowd was rowdy and drunk. An Eastern European brass band played a mix of Western pop—Michael Jackson, the Police, Imagine Dragons—and Ukrainian pop classics, including my favorite Ukrainian song, the seventies hit "Chervona Ruta." I'd first heard the song performed by a four-piece brass band on Lesya Ukrainka in Lutsk. Dima had told me that the song was about a rhododendron, and also maybe that it was a metaphor for a woman, and that it was popular with his parents' generation. When the opening refrain rolled in at the beer hall, the crowd went nuts and started banging bottles against their tables in rhythm. The chorus was deafening, two hundred people belting it out, with the over-forty crowd singing with the passion of soldiers who'd just won a battle. The reaction reminded me of that to "Sweet Caroline" or "Don't Stop Believin'." I sang along with the chorus in Ukrainian, which, besides a few mumbled phrases, I knew by heart. I was pleased to see Muriel look down, not knowing the words. I had the impulse to implore her to sing along, but why be a dick. Instead, when it went back into the verse, I leaned over and said, ". . . and those are the only lyrics I know to any Ukrainian song."

She laughed. "I've never heard it before—but it's really catchy!"

It might have been that one moment of connection, or it might have been the music—the great thing about live music was that you could be with someone without talking to them all the time—or it might have been the third beer I was on, but I started enjoying myself. When Muriel leaned over to kiss me, I kissed her back, and it felt kind of nice. She smiled at me and we went back to watching the band.

It would be nice to enjoy another body for a night, wouldn't it? And, really, what good would more abstinence do? What had I learned from four months of it? That I was pretty much the same person abstinent as when I was having sex—only with slightly less guilt and anxiety.

But then the band started playing "Satisfaction," and my thoughts found their way to my father, who loved the Rolling Stones. He'd seen them live as a teenager in the sixties and then about two dozen times since—twice with me. I remembered the way his face lit up at the first notes of "Jumpin' Jack Flash" pounding through Dodger Stadium when I was sixteen. The way he looked over to see if I was excited about the song, too. Then I couldn't stop thinking about how much I wanted to bring my dad to Ukraine. He would have loved it—the strange adventure of it all. I probably wouldn't have invited him to come, as the logistics of getting him here and figuring out how to spend all that time together would have been a headache. But the thought of just spending an evening with him, here, now, in this bar—or not even an evening, just a moment, listening to this Ukrainian band play "Satisfaction" . . .

Muriel looked like she was going to kiss me again. But the thought of having to be close to someone who'd never met my father was too much. I excused myself to the bathroom. I felt silly, self-indulgent, and very sad. When I came back, I couldn't locate any of the energy from just minutes earlier. Everything was dark.

Muriel was talking about a friend who had stayed on in Kyiv after finishing his Peace Corps stint in 2014. That friend had participated in the Maidan protests in what sounded like a performative and touristic kind of way. Muriel said that he had been chasing the rush ever since.

"Nothing's ever going to be as good as Maidan," she said.

It was such a stupid story. She didn't seem to realize how shallow her friend sounded for treating something so important like it was bungee jumping.

"Let's head back," I said.

"Already?" she said. "It's barely midnight."

"I'm beat."

"Come on! Don't be boring." It was hard to tell if she was being flirtatious or mean, or hiding the latter beneath the former.

"You can stay if you want. But I'm beat."

"I'm not going to stay here alone."

I shrugged. "Okay."

I paid the bill and she put on her coat in a huff and didn't talk to me on the twenty-minute walk back to the apartment.

"I'm not having sex with you," she said after we got inside.

I shrugged. "I'll sleep on the couch."

"You don't have to sleep on the couch. Don't be dramatic. It's a big bed."

"Okay," I said neutrally.

In bed, she huffed and tossed and turned, clearly waiting for me to say something, but I had nothing to say. I just wanted to go home.

Soon she snuggled up and started kissing me.

"I don't understand. I thought you didn't want to."

"Just stop talking," she said, and kissed me more. "You're better when you don't talk."

I pushed her away.

"What's wrong with you?" she said.

"You said you didn't want to, so we're not going to. I'm tired. I'm going to sleep."

"This trip cost me a lot of money, you know. I can't just gallivant around like you."

It was true that I made a lot more money than she did—and probably did less work to earn it. But we had each made our choices. And I had paid for everything except for half the apartment and the bus ticket from her house to the Lutsk bus station. All in all, she'd spent less than twenty-five dollars on the whole trip.

I got up, retrieved my wallet, and took out all the cash I had—about eighty dollars' worth of hryvnias—and put it on the table. "Here."

"Jesus Christ! I'm not a fucking beggar."

"I'm just reimbursing you."

"I wasn't asking for reimbursement."

"Okay, fine," I said. "I'm not reimbursing you. I'm paying you."

When I would think about this moment later, there would be shame—that familiar cringe that made me shut my eyes and clench my teeth and kept me awake at night. But there would also be another feeling—something like triumph.

She looked at me with anger but also curiosity. Like maybe this was a game I was inviting her into. "You're paying me?" she said. "For what?"

"To stop talking."

She glared at me for several seconds with hatred; I looked back with indifference. Finally, she got into bed and turned off the light. I slept on the couch. When I woke in the morning, the money was gone from the table. The only things we said to each other for the rest of the day were, "Did you order the taxi?," "Did you lock the door?," "Is this our bus?," and "Bye." It was a shitty thing to do. I knew that. But she wouldn't stop pushing. I needed her to stop pushing. And it had worked. If she'd thought I was better when I didn't talk, then I wouldn't talk. But she wouldn't be talking either.

Since then, with the office closed for the holiday break, my days had been far too empty, and with nothing else with which to occupy myself, I kept revisiting how I'd acted with Muriel. Every time I thought about it, it got worse. At the same time, I couldn't apologize, because I didn't want to see her again, which could be the next step if she accepted my apology.

The trip to Lviv had also unlocked something dangerous in my brain: the knowledge that just because I had said I was going to be abstinent for a year didn't mean I had to stick to it. If I didn't want to complicate things in Lutsk, where everyone seemed to be watching me all the time, I could go back to Lviv to try to meet someone. They had dating apps in Ukraine, too, and Lviv suddenly felt like an option now that I knew how to get there and navigate the city. It was a choice I didn't want, and its presence doubled my anxiety. I needed another voice to interrupt me. To say so what if I had been an asshole to Muriel? She had also been an asshole to me. To say that it was fine to stay in Lutsk and keep living the life I'd been living—that life would surely feel good again once the holidays ended. But I had returned from Lviv the day before Ukrainian Christmas, and everyone I knew was gone. Each day back passed slower and slower. Every hour was stretched out by the knowledge that I wouldn't be seeing anyone else for days. But then late last night, Davey had called. I'd never felt so happy to see his name on my phone.

"Turner! What's good, my guy?"

"Just enjoying the tropical Ukrainian winter."

"I can see it now. White sand beaches. Girls in bikinis. Polar bears."

"You're not too far off."

I asked him how things were back home, and he talked about the business and this girl he'd just started seeing, whom he'd met on Instagram and who had the best real tits he'd ever encountered.

"That must be great for you," I said, probably a little weirdly, but trying to conceal any judgment, even though the college bragging felt embarrassingly out of place in an adult conversation. Mostly it was just nice to hear a familiar voice.

He asked how things were with me.

"You know, they're good. I'm just—" I found myself about to tell him about Muriel. But then I was preemptively ashamed of what I was going to reveal. "I'll be honest with you. I don't know what I'm doing with the agents. I worry that I'm not getting through to them. Do you have any tips?" I put my face in my hand. This was not what I wanted at all: getting advice from Davey for a problem I didn't need help with in the first place.

"Yeah, absolutely," he said. "My advice is to stop being such a dumb shit."

"What?"

"Look, I hate to say this, because you're just about the smartest guy I know, but that's about the dumbest shit I've ever heard. I've read the assessments. You're doing a great job. They're getting way better."

"But I'm the one writing the assessments." I had no idea why I was arguing with him, but I couldn't stop myself. "Don't you think that's a conflict of interest?"

"I sure don't. We're about to start sending the customer surveys out, and I'm sure they'll confirm what you've already told me. But besides that, why would you lie to me? You're on the phone trying to convince me that you're bad at your job, and you think I'm worried about you padding your stats? Come on, my guy. Your biggest problem is that you don't know how to frame things positively—for other people or for yourself."

I thought my biggest problem was probably my personality, followed closely by my decisions. But it sounded like he was going to say nice things about me, so I let him go on.

"You think everything's going so badly. But you moved to Ukraine, sight unseen, and turned this ship around, in what, four months? You're my guy. Just stop being so fucking hard on yourself."

Back in college, after a girlfriend and I had broken up, Davey had come over once and brought me a Whopper meal, claiming that it was a two-for-one deal at Burger King. We hadn't talked about the breakup at all, but I knew there was no two-for-one deal. It wasn't like buying me a hamburger had been such a big deal. But I still remembered it as the most tender thing any of my male friends had done in college.

When Davey was satisfied that he'd convinced me to stay on in Lutsk, we got off the phone, and I thought about how much better I felt than I had before he called, even though I hadn't even mentioned any of the stuff I'd been thinking about. Then I put in my earplugs and slept the best sleep I'd slept all week.

So when I'd woken this morning from that wonderful sleep, it was with renewed energy and no idea that I would be spending the day visiting ATMs. I bundled up, put on my basketball podcast, and, with a bouncier feeling than I'd had all break, headed off to the store for bread and juice and maybe some chocolate. But as I came down the stairs to the landing, Natalia opened the front door. She was carrying a paper shopping bag—from a boutique rather than the grocery store—and staring off into nothing. Maybe her eyes were adjusting from the brightness of the snow to the darkness of the stairwell. Maybe her mind was elsewhere. Either way, she didn't see me. She was hatless, despite the cold, and looked beautiful with her rosy cheeks and snow-dotted hair. She undid her scarf. On her throat were two yellow-and-black bruises. One on each side. She snapped back from wherever she was, saw me, and quickly wrapped the scarf back around her throat.

"Good morning, John," she said in a trembling voice.

He had choked her.

"Are you okay?" I said.

"Yes, of course," she said, nodding and looking off to the side.

"What happened?"

"It's nothing."

"Let me help you."

"Please," she said dismissively with a wave of her hand. She might have thought that I meant help her with her bag, but I meant help her not get killed.

"We need to get you out of here. Is there somewhere you can go? I can give you the money."

"I have money," she said neutrally.

"You can stay at my place. I mean, I could sleep on the couch. Or I could stay somewhere else and you could have my apartment."

"I'm going to my sister's."

"Good. That's a good idea."

"I'm having dinner there. Anatoly is working until evening, so he will not join me. I will play with her children. I bought presents for them." She held up her bag. "Then I will return home. And then, next week, I will see you at work. Goodbye, John."

And she was gone again. She didn't want my help. But she was getting terrorized in there. I couldn't call the police. I couldn't reason with Anatoly—even if we had spoken the same language, I couldn't have reasoned with him. I didn't think trying to fight him would do any good. I'd been boxing for a while now, but who knew if I would win, and even if I did, what would that accomplish? I couldn't be there with her 24/7 and pissing him off and then leaving was probably the worst thing I could do to her. Just pounding on the door to let him know that I was there hadn't worked—he had choked her anyway. I had been sleeping peacefully while he choked her. He could've killed her.

I went to the store in a daze and came home without remembering anything I'd bought. I paced around the apartment all morning wondering what to do. I grew so tired of the sound of my thoughts that I began to think that doing anything would be better than this continued nothing.

And that was when it had hit me. Once the thought arrived, it was so obvious. I would pay him to stop hitting Natalia. Anatoly probably made 7,000 or 8,000 hryvnias per month. I would offer him 50,000 hryvnias to stop hitting his wife. I would stuff an envelope so full of bills that it wouldn't even close. He'd still be recovering from the shock when I told him that there was another envelope just as full coming his way in three months if Natalia went unharmed. Together, those two envelopes would be more than a year of his salary. He couldn't refuse that kind of money. Nor could I think of another way to spend the money that would feel anywhere close to as good as this would. I was doing something—finally, I was actually doing something.

Now, on my way to the sixth ATM of the day, I crossed through a park I'd never visited near the Promin shopping center. The sun was shining down too weakly to send any heat but strongly enough to wax the ground, and I stepped cautiously. There was a giant monument at the center of the park, a tower of black marble several stories high, far too grand for its surroundings. I stopped to read what I could of the monument, which was dedicated to those who died fighting the Germans. I struggled to imagine what it was like to grow up with this history—with a monument to those who fought the Nazis, even though some of those who fought the Nazis also tried to starve you to death. I wondered what it did to someone to grow up with the memory of war on your home soil between two armies that wanted to kill you. With the legacy of government-sanctioned famine that killed millions, then war-caused famine that killed countless more. To grow up under dictatorship and secret police, where even a kind word from a stranger could be a trap. And then, once freedom came, to live under lawlessness and stifling corruption. Maybe violence was a price you were willing to pay for stability. Or maybe there wasn't much of a choice.

I started walking again and imagined what would happen when Anatoly got home from work and I knocked on his door. I got so deep into the fantasy—what I would say and how Anatoly would respond, and whether, given how closely the Ukrainians at the office seemed to track my movements, everyone would quickly learn what I had done—that I didn't see Dima until he was right in front of me.

"John! You are thinking too hard!"

We shook hands and our gloves made a muffled thud when they met. Dima said he was just out for a walk and that it was great to run into another crazy person who wanted to walk in this weather. I was surprised at how happy I was to see him. Not that I didn't normally like seeing Dima. But today it felt like an absolute blessing.

I told him that I needed to stop at a couple ATMs to withdraw cash. But when I revealed how much cash I needed, Dima took me to a foreign bank that I'd never heard of, which let you make large withdrawals.

"Are you buying something?" Dima said as I put the cash in my wallet, too embarrassed to hide this bunch.

"It's difficult to use an American card in Ukraine. I like having a lot of cash handy." Which was basically true. My bank had frozen my credit card four times already for no other reason than that a computer periodically considered it suspicious to be in Ukraine. "But I am buying something, too."

"What are you buying?"

"A round of beers for us."

Dima took a second to process the information. "This is very generous. But to be honest, I can't drink alcohol for one year."

"New Year's resolution?"

"What?"

"Why can't you drink alcohol for one year?"

"I was bitten by a dog. I have to take medicine, so no alcohol for one year."

"Oh my god. Are you okay? What happened?"

"I'm fine. I was bitten by a dog."

After more prodding, as we turned onto Prospekt Prezydenta Hrushevskoho, Dima explained that he'd been out for a walk one day when a dog on a leash jumped up and bit him on the leg. The bite tore through his pants and his skin and he thought it wasn't a big deal, but when he told his mother she said that he had to go to the hospital immediately. When he went to the hospital, the doctor said that he had to track down the woman who owned the dog to have it tested for rabies.

"But how am I to find this woman? I have never seen her before today."

He required treatment in case the dog did have rabies. The doctor told him that he could either spend two weeks in the hospital receiving treatment or get one shot that afternoon, then go home and then take pills for one year. Dima didn't want to spend two weeks laid up, so he chose the take-home option.

"At first, going to the hospital to be treated for rabies was a little bit outside my comfort zone," he said. "But near the hospital was a beautiful lake and white hills. They had clean rooms, and they gave me food. And then it wasn't outside my comfort zone because it was comfortable."

What amazed me wasn't that Dima was so upbeat—or that it was a leashed dog rather than a stray that had been his downfall—but that I had to pry every detail of the story out of him. It wasn't embarrassment or hesitancy to talk about it that I sensed—he just didn't seem to think it was interesting.

"It wasn't the New Year's holiday I was hoping for," he admitted. "But then I thought to myself, there must be a reason this happened. For example, yesterday I went out dancing. Usually, when I go out dancing, I drink some beer. Yesterday, I had juice instead. It was just as fun to go dancing without beer. And today, when I woke up, I felt great. My mind was ready to go. Now I have been walking around all day thinking of ideas for my speech."

"What speech?"

"I didn't tell you? I am giving a speech on Facebook to a group of American entrepreneurs about starting businesses in Ukraine."

"Congratulations!"

We cut back toward the city center, and Dima asked if I had any advice about speaking to an American audience.

"The most classic advice for giving speeches in America is to start with a joke."

"I understand. What kind of joke?"

"Something funny, hopefully."

"This is not very helpful, John." He laughed. "Maybe my joke about Ukraine? 'Let me introduce you to the neighbors!'"

"I like that joke, but it might be a little bit too long to start with." I did like the joke, but when Dima told it, it took about five minutes to get to the punch line. "The point of starting with a joke is to make the audience trust you quickly. If they trust you, they'll relax, because they're not tense from the fear that you're going to be terrible. And few things create trust quicker than showing you have a sense of humor."

"This is good to know. But frankly speaking, John, I don't think I know any quick jokes."

"Well, how about this: One way to create trust through humor is through self-deprecation. Do you know this phrase? I don't know what it's called in Ukrainian, but in some languages it's called 'self-irony.' It's showing that you can laugh at yourself."

Dima nodded.

"The first thing your American audience is going to notice about you is that you have an Eastern European accent. It's unavoidable. So you could make a joke about that. You could say, 'I am currently a software developer and an entrepreneur with my own brand of earplugs. Before that, I spent several years trying to kill James Bond.'"

"I don't understand."

I felt my face getting a little hot. "Unfortunately, the first thing Americans are going to think of when they hear an Eastern European accent is a movie villain, like you'd see in a James Bond movie. Because that's where the most Americans have been exposed to Eastern European accents. I think it started as Cold War propaganda, and then just kind of became a popular thing to do in action movies." I paused. "I'm sorry. It's a stupid stereotype. We're just kind of stupid."

"No, no! This is good to know. I understand now. I will use this joke. 'Before that I spent several years trying to kill James Bond.' They will laugh, and I will create trust. Thank you, John."

We stopped into a small café for a coffee to warm up. Dima ordered and insisted on paying. We sat down, and I felt my toes, ears, and nose tingling back to life.

"How is the American girl?" Dima said. "Have you seen her again?"

"Yes, we went to Lviv together."

"To Lviv? What a fantastic date. You are very romantic."

"It wasn't great."

"Why not?"

The question made me feel a little alone, though there was another person right there. "I don't think we're a good match. She talks too loudly. We go into a restaurant and she's practically screaming. It's embarrassing."

"But when your voice is loud, you're powerful."

"Maybe."

"No, it's true. When your voice is loud, it means you're free. Maybe this is why Americans talk loudly—because you are free."

"I think that's a very generous interpretation."

"I don't understand."

"I mean to say that I think you are being very kind to loud Americans. I think that when your voice is loud and everyone else is speaking quietly, but you keep speaking loudly, it means that you are free, but it also means that you are rude. That you either do not have any awareness of the people around you or you just don't care about them."

He shrugged. "Maybe. But maybe Americans do not need awareness. America has the smartest people, John. It has the most money, the best of everything. So you get to talk loudly."

I smiled. "I really hope that's not the case."

We headed back toward the center. On Prospekt Voli, we passed a beautiful blond woman in a peacoat, stockings, and high heels, holding hands with what looked like a balding warehouse worker in track pants and a puffer jacket.

"Have you noticed," I said, after a short internal debate that ended with me telling myself that Dima and I were friends now and that friends are allowed to make mistakes and say stupid things to each other, "that women here are often better looking than their husbands?"

Dima looked at me like I had said something ridiculous. "Often? Always!" He laughed. "It is a wonderful situation!"

"I didn't know if it was something Ukrainians noticed, too," I said, relieved.

"Yes, certainly. It's the best part about Ukraine." He laughed. "When I was in Germany, it was the exact opposite situation. The German men are tall and beautiful, and the women are not so beautiful. The whole time I was there, I don't think a single woman looked at me. But here, when I go dancing, I never have a dance free. It's a wonderful situation."

We turned into the main square. The massive tree that stood in front of the monument to those who died at Maidan and the local soldiers killed in the war in the east had been decorated for the season with yards of tinsel and lights. It shone cheerfully in the darkness.

"I will go home now to eat dinner," Dima said.

I didn't want to be alone again. But I realized that my legs were tired and I was hungry, too.

Dima insisted on walking me to my building.

"You live on this street?" Dima said.

"I do."

"It is as I said: Americans must be free!"

I laughed a little. "Sorry, I don't understand."

"It was joke. You live on Prospekt Voli. It means 'Avenue of Freedom.'" He chuckled a little at himself. "Stupid joke. But tell me, John, are you missing your home?"

The question caught me off guard. Something inside me melted a little. Maybe I just needed to eat.

"Normally I don't miss it that much. But now that you mention it, I guess I have been missing it a little around the holidays."

"Your heart hurts, being away?"

I thought of my dad, swearing in the kitchen, always burning his hands on something. He made the best gravy, thick and rich with sherry. "In America it's called being homesick. And yes, I am a little homesick."

"Homesick," Dima repeated.

We reached the building's front door and shook hands goodbye.

"I hope that your homesickness feels better," Dima said.

"Thank you. I hope you don't have rabies."

I trudged up the steps slowly. I stopped outside Natalia's apartment to listen but heard no sounds. Anatoly wasn't home yet. I missed the sounds of neighbors laughing and yelling words in English. The sound of basketball on the TV. Of my dad yelling, "What?" from whatever room he was in. In the kitchen, I ripped off a slightly hardened piece of the morning's baguette, cut a chunk of dry salami from its log, and washed it down with a beer. Then I opened the bourbon left over from the New Year's Eve party and poured a healthy glass.

I pulled up the translation page I'd bookmarked on my computer and practiced.

I have a proposal for you.

U mene ye propozytsiya dlya vas.

Stop hitting her.

Perestan' byty yiyi.

I will pay you.

Ya vam zaplachu.

Then, after a dramatic pause: Fifty thousand hryvnias.

P'yatdesyat tysyach hryven'.

I pulled the wads of bills from their hiding places across my body. Four months in Ukraine and I'd never witnessed or heard of anyone being robbed—but still. I finagled the stack of 200-hryvnia notes into a small white envelope. It was such a thick stack, so much money. I had earned this money, through my work, through my mind, which a businessman with money had deemed valuable enough to pay me for.

Its absence would have no effect on my life whatsoever. How strange, how emboldening, to be rich. I felt bigger than I'd ever felt before. I'd pull the envelope from my back pocket and hold it out to Anatoly. But before giving it to him, I'd say, "*Bil'she ne bude nasyl'stva.*" No more violence.

But what if Anatoly didn't take the money? What if he attacked me? Unlikely. Who attacked a man offering you a year's salary? But if he did, I'd be ready. I practiced ducking left in anticipation of Anatoly's right, then rising into a left hook to destabilize him, and then coming in with a hard-right uppercut. That would catch him under the chin, and I could get away. If that happened, I would have to warn Natalia before she got home. But it wouldn't happen. Nevertheless, I practiced the combination in the kitchen. Duck, three, roll, four, run out the door. Duck, three, roll, four, run out the door. Just as I was getting out of breath, I saw through the window Anatoly passing under a streetlamp in the courtyard. He was wearing a puffer jacket and work pants, smoking a cigarette. He stopped to pet a stray. I wished he hadn't done that.

I heard the front door open. Labored steps going up the stairs.

I had another drink. Then another. I felt a little elsewhere. But also fired up. Very fired up. I was going to do something. Anatoly was not going to hit her anymore. I put on my boots. Brushed my teeth. Practiced my words in the mirror, then my punches. The words felt a little mixed up. I might have drunk too much. But at least my voice sounded deep and emotionless, like a Ukrainian. I ran through the punches one last time.

I stepped into the hall. Took a deep breath. Their front door was different from mine. Mine had ornate carvings on dark wood. Theirs was lighter, cheaper-looking wood, with plaster filled in on the top where the door didn't fit the doorway. I knocked. Waited.

Anatoly opened. Betrayed no expression. Wore a thick sweater. His hair was receding a little on the sides but hung down over his forehead boyishly. He was a little shorter than me but broad. Strong. Smelled surprisingly good—like he was wearing expensive cologne.

"*Dobryi vechir,*" I said.

"*Dobryi vechir,*" he said.

He stepped aside and motioned me in.

"*Bud' laska,*" he said.

I started to take off my boots, but halfway through I wondered if this would be seen as a sign of weakness. But Anatoly wasn't wearing shoes. So it would be rude to leave mine on. Or would it look strong? I felt a little dizzy.

Now shoeless, I followed Anatoly into the living room. It was so full of old furniture that it was hard to navigate. Cabinets, armoires, chairs with faded upholstery, a green couch with wooden armrests. In the middle of the room, a large square coffee table with a thick glass top. Everything looked dusty, but when I discreetly ran my finger over a shelf it came back clean.

I didn't know if I was supposed to sit down or if he was going to offer me something to drink or if we were just going to talk standing up. The quiet was getting unbearable.

I blurted out: "*U mene ye propozytsiya dlya vas.*"

Anatoly didn't say anything. His face suggested that a child just told him he had a proposition. He looked curious but mostly amused.

I felt my anger rising quickly, too quickly, and I jumped into the next phrase: "*Zaymatysya seksom zi mnoyu.*"

Anatoly frowned. "*What?*" he said, in Ukrainian.

"*Zaymatysya seksom zi mnoyu,*" I said, then quickly added, "*Ya vam zaplachu.*"

"*You'll pay me?*" Anatoly repeated in Ukrainian. His face turned red.

I forgot the whole order of operations and said, in Ukrainian, "*Certainly, certainly I will pay you. Fifty thousand hryvnias. Yes? But—*" Anatoly pushed me. I fell backwards into a shelf. I kept my footing, stood back up. "Take it easy!" I yelled in English.

Anatoly yelled something in Ukrainian that I didn't understand. I got my stance square and put my fists up. Anatoly charged toward me. I ducked. Threw the left hook. Missed completely. Rolled under the punch that never arrived. Threw the right uppercut. Made contact. Hit Anatoly's chin, hard. Hit it earlier, lower than expected. Like he was diving into it. He screamed. The pain shot through my wrist and up to my elbow. Anatoly crashed into the table. The glass cracked terribly. He was on the floor. Bleeding.

I froze. Tried to catch my breath. Knelt down. "Anatoly?" There was blood coming out from the back of his head. "Hey, Anatoly." I put my hand under his nose and felt him breathing. I put my finger on his throat and felt the pulse beating. I pulled out my phone and, hands shaking, googled *head injury*.

Call 911. Keep the person still. Stop the bleeding.

I took my scarf and wedged it gently under the head where it was bleeding. I pressed the scarf against the wound. It was bad. Very bad.

"Come on, Anatoly," I said in a soft voice. "You're okay."

I was shaking all over now. But I could do this. It was okay. Anatoly was breathing, steadily. People don't breathe steadily when they're not okay. I'd apply the pressure until the bleeding stopped. Then I would call the police. Say I heard a break-in.

But Anatoly would contradict that. As soon as he woke up. I would go to Ukrainian prison. Images from a movie about a captured British Cold War spy flashed before me: head shaved, marched naked into a cell with no mattress, sleep-deprivation lights overhead, freezing in an unheated room with no coat, woken in the night for interrogations. It wouldn't be like that. This wasn't the Soviet Union and I wasn't a spy. But what would it be like?

One thing at a time.

Stop the bleeding. Make sure Anatoly was breathing okay. Call an ambulance. Then leave. Not just the apartment but leave Lutsk. Leave Ukraine. I held the scarf in place. I felt the blood warming my hand. After a few minutes I checked the wound. The bleeding had already slowed. It wasn't gushing. The blood was starting to coagulate. It was getting better. It was bad, but not that bad. A concussion. A bad gash. But it was getting better.

Stop the bleeding. Call the ambulance. Then leave the country.

Or be arrested and go to Ukrainian prison.

I leaned down to examine the wound again. A deep cut, to be sure. But you couldn't see bone. And the borders of a dark scab, almost black, were already forming. I felt under his nose. He was breathing regularly. Strong breaths. I felt his pulse again. Same as before. Normal. Maybe. I didn't know what normal was. I compared it to my own, but my heart was beating a thousand beats a second. The early-morning train to Lviv. It would still be dark out. Then a morning flight to Warsaw. Then Warsaw to LA. Or I could call a taxi to take me to Lviv now. But first the bleeding. Then the ambulance. Then—

Through the window, under the streetlamp, coming through the courtyard, was Natalia.

Oh no.

No more time to think. Make a decision. I had acted in defense of Natalia. Anatoly was the one who had resorted to violence; I would have left if he asked. Anatoly was the one who led us down this path.

I carefully removed the scarf and gently set Anatoly's head down. I took his wallet from his pocket. I used my jacket to wipe down the parts on and around Anatoly that I might have touched. I grabbed my shoes, hurried out the door, wiped down the doorknob, left the door slightly ajar, and snuck back into my apartment. There was blood on my hands and face in the mirror. I washed it off. The water turned red in the sink. Natalia's footsteps came up the stairs. Stopped outside her door.

"Anatoly?" she said. "Anatoly?"

Anatoly's back was killing him. He'd woken up stiff for no good reason—but since when did pain need a reason? Every time he moved, it hurt. He drove to the first address on the day's delivery sheet—every slot booked, of course—stepped out from the van into the cold, heaved an ice-cold 19-liter jug of water onto his shoulder, and let out an involuntary grunt. He punched in the door code with his free hand. He climbed seventy-eight steps to the fourth floor, every step agony. He knocked on the door. An old woman answered. He set her jug down in the kitchen. She gave him fifty hryvnias. He handed her a receipt and four hryvnias back.

As he walked down the stairs, taking a little pleasure at the absence of the weight on his shoulder, he recalled how, when he was younger—when he began this job that had at some point between then and now become a life—his problem was boredom. But over the years, it had morphed into the much less intellectual problem of pain. His knees. His hips. His back. There was nothing interesting to say about physical pain the way there was with boredom, angst, or emotional pain. Physical pain was the analogy you used to describe psychological torment. *When she died, it broke my heart.* What then was the metaphor for physical pain? *When my back hurt, it was like being annoyed with everybody all the time.* No, that was traveling in the wrong direction, trivializing instead of elevating. The only way to describe physical pain was through other physical pain. Everyone knew that it hurt like hell to be shot, but it wasn't until Anatoly heard a soldier on the news describe the burning feeling that came from the bullet, the worst burning of your life, that he could start to imagine what it actually felt like to be shot.

His back ached, but it didn't burn. It felt like stiff wood—wood that needed to be water. It was painful that the wood could not be water. But it was no use. Physical pain was just pain, insistent and without poetry. Yet when it was present, it was all there was. How frustrating to be consumed by something so uninteresting.

He opened the door to the courtyard. He saw Dmitry's boy, Misha, standing near the van, posing for a selfie in front of the snow-covered trees. How old was he now? Eleven? Twelve?

"Misha! You look like a woman."

Misha looked up, startled, then saw that it was just Anatoly. "I look handsome. You're just jealous."

"We'll get you some high heels and the effect will be complete. But why aren't you in school?"

"There's no school today would be the main reason."

"You're a bad liar," Anatoly said, realizing, as he said it, that as it was only three days after Christmas, there was a real prospect that there was no school today. Just because he didn't get a holiday didn't mean others would be similarly deprived. "Go to school—they'll teach you to lie better."

"If they taught us to lie, I'd go to school every day, even weekends. I could be president one day! But we just have to write reports about old castles."

"But how will you succeed in this world if you don't know about old castles?" Anatoly lit a cigarette. For the first time today, he was enjoying himself. "If we don't know the past, we are bound to repeat it."

"What does that even mean?"

"It means that if you don't learn about castles, you're bound to build one. And what use does anyone have for a castle these days?"

Misha laughed.

"Besides, if you don't go to school, you'll end up like me, doing work better suited for a beast than a man."

"But didn't you go to school?"

"I did."

"To university?"

"Not only to university—but to the second-best university in all of Lutsk!"

"But there are only two universities in Lutsk."

"And I went to the second-best! If you want to learn how to study philosophy, there is no finer institute of higher education."

Misha giggled. "But you're a deliveryman. Work better suited for a beast."

"Or a philosopher, Misha. My occupation gives me plenty of time to think."

"But if you studied philosophy, why don't you work as a philosopher?"

"Well, the answer to that is twofold. When I finished university, things were a little different than they are now. It was harder than the world you've been lucky enough to inherit. At the time, the only way to get a good job was to know the right people. It didn't matter your skill—only your connections. With that in mind, the first problem was that I had no connections, and without connections, there was no hope of becoming a professional philosopher. The second problem," he said, and took a drag, "is that there is no such thing as a professional philosopher."

Misha laughed. "Then why did you study philosophy?"

"You bring up a valid point. Maybe university is not the answer." He feigned thinking. "All right, here's my revised advice: marry an ugly woman with lots of money."

"But you didn't marry an ugly woman with lots of money."

"Exactly! I married a beautiful woman with no money!" Though it would be more accurate to say that she had once been a beautiful woman with no money and was now a slightly less beautiful woman who made a lot of money. "But she did come with an apartment, which I must say is a great advantage. Did your mother come with an apartment?"

"Ask her yourself."

"Tell me, please, do I look like I want to die?"

The boy laughed. Anatoly couldn't remember the last time he'd made Natalia laugh. If they had a child, the child would probably find him funny. Children usually did.

"Heed my words, Misha: Marry the ugliest woman you can find. And tell your father that he owes me lunch." He put out his cigarette and tossed a fifty-kopeck coin to the boy. "Back to work for this beast. Go to school now and buy yourself something nice on the way."

"What am I supposed to buy with fifty kopecks?"

"Two twenty-five-kopeck coins. Or five ten-kopeck coins! The possibilities are endless!"

Anatoly rode the high of that fun until the next delivery, when his foul mood returned. Three flights of stairs, another ugly old lady, another gauntlet from the heat of the van to the bitter cold outside, to the milder cold of the stairwell, to the stifling torture chamber of the hot apartment, and then the whole thing in reverse.

He was reminded, not for the first time, of Sisyphus, who, as Camus pointed out, wasn't tragic because he had to roll the same rock up the same hill for all eternity. Sisyphus was tragic because he *knew* he had to roll the rock up the same hill. If Sisyphus didn't know that the rock would always tumble back down—if, say, his memory was wiped clean after every trip up the mountain and as he neared the peak he experienced hope and relief at nearing the completion of the task—then where was the tragedy? It was the knowledge of his futility that made him tragic. Anatoly, like Sisyphus, was painfully aware of his fate. Only he no longer took pleasure in his tragedy. It was more fun to be tragic when you were young—or at least sitting down. But did Natalia appreciate it?

Stop, he told himself. It was too early in the day for all that.

The worrying part about the backache, Anatoly thought as he got behind the wheel and checked the sheet for his next delivery, was that it was increasing in frequency. When he was younger, his back would turn to wood every so often—maybe for a day or two when he returned from holiday and his muscles had lain dormant for too long. But now the backache arrived every month. Instead of lasting for a day or two, it would linger for four or five days. He was only thirty-eight—this was too early for his body to start breaking. He wondered if this was his future: watching the days that were full of pain overtaking the pain-free days a little more each year until there was nothing left but pain.

He wanted to suffer in silence. He wanted to handle it stoically so everyone would see how stoic he was. But the problem was that Natalia would never notice that he was suffering in silence unless he told her. Now, his mother—she would notice right away. She could see it in his eyes. Every time he squinted, she asked if he was all right. But Natalia only knew if he told her, and if he told her she would think he was a malingerer. It was a catch-22. She would only know of his pain if he told her; but if he told her, she would not believe him to be in pain. These problems were funnier in literature. In the actual *Catch-22*, the soldier Yossarian can only be sent home from war if he's declared insane. But he can only be declared insane if he asks for an evaluation of his sanity; and if he asks for an evaluation of his sanity so that he can go home, it's proof that he's sane—because only a crazy person would want to stay and fight. Whatever Yossarian does, he must stay and fight. Whatever Anatoly did, he had to suffer without his wife's sympathy.

His mother had warned him not to marry that girl. His father would have liked her, because she was beautiful and his father had liked beautiful things—often talked about how much more beautiful the women were back home in Russia. Natalia had been not only beautiful—and still was beautiful—but also not at all boring. And since she was the oldest and her parents had their own house outside the city, she had inherited a nice two-room apartment in the center from her grandparents.

"You'll be forever standing in water with nothing to drink," his mother had warned.

"Somebody's jealous, somebody's jealous," Anatoly sang out as he wrapped his mother in a hug from behind.

"Stop it! I'm trying to cook, Anatoly!"

Anatoly's "somebody's jealous" song morphed into "Chervona Ruta." He broke into the chorus and forced his mother into a herky-jerky dance. She gasped through her laughter, "Anatoly! You are too much, you bandit!"

He stopped dancing and looked down at her, that beautiful stout little woman who had endured so much to bring him into the world. "Mother, you know that you will always be my favorite girl."

"You are a good boy," she'd said, with tears in her eyes.

Maybe this was the problem. His mother was still his favorite girl. He loved his wife—but he didn't always like her. He always liked his mother.

A yellow light began blinking on his dashboard. *Check engine. Check engine.* Like a nerve blinking in his back. *Fuck this day. Fuck the engine. Let Alexei deal with it.*

To be fair to Natalia, and to himself and the decisions he'd made, he often liked his wife. She was funny—funnier than any other woman he'd met. She did excellent impressions and could pull off any number of accents. She teased him in a way that showed how well she knew him and filled him with delight. And she used to laugh at his jokes, sincerely, heartily, taking great pleasure in them. Sometimes they would lie in bed taking turns drawing out a joke together, more and more, until there was no juice left to squeeze. They would lie there gasping, out of breath from laughing. He would think that this was what it must be like working with a great philosopher on a proof. Or with a great actor on a scene. Or standing on the stage of a smoky jazz club in Chicago with a great saxophonist as they improvised off each other to the delight of the crowd.

But she could also be cruel. It wasn't until he met Natalia that he learned that he wasn't good at everything. In school, at home, at university—he'd always excelled. Everyone thought he was the smartest, the funniest, the best. But his wife pointed out numerous flaws. At first, he thought that she was just being kind of a bitch, as wives were known to be. But her arguments proving his faults were so good that he couldn't even argue back. Which meant either that she was right about him not being good at everything or that he was not as good at arguing as he had previously thought. Either way, she'd proven that he wasn't good at everything, since even the second option would mean he wasn't good at arguing. He knew that she was disappointed in what he'd become—or failed to become. But how dare she? It wasn't as if he'd had a choice. The way she'd looked at him last night—like he was a joke. Since when was a decade of sacrifice for your family a joke?

Maybe the problem was that they weren't a family. They were just a couple. He suspected that having children might make his wife less dissatisfied: less focused on the things that made her unhappy and more focused on the joy of keeping a very cute little person alive. But she wasn't eager to have kids—not yet at least. She wanted to wait until they had lived a little more. They'd lived a lot now—or they'd at least lived a long time. The time was coming to have kids—had come and gone already, actually. But he couldn't remember the last time they'd talked about it. She was still on the pill, not that she had much need for it lately, and though he'd never admit it out loud, part of him was relieved, since he wasn't even sure he wanted to have kids. What if they turned out stupid or dull? Or if they were girls? He wasn't eager for more girls in the house. Frankly, it was lucky that Natalia was so hesitant, because this way he could blame her when his mother asked why there were no children. And he would say this in Natalia's defense: despite everything, she was not the least bit scared of his mother.

"But wouldn't you like a son? A little boy of your own?" his mother would prod.

"Maybe once yours is grown," Natalia said. "Right now I have my hands full with him."

His mother certainly didn't appreciate that. But how could a person even argue that that was not funny? It was *objectively funny* when Natalia answered his mother that way. Come on.

He delivered another jug, then another one. Every wretched jug he had to hoist from the floor of the van to his shoulder tightened his back further. With every turn of the screw, he'd hear his wife's disbelief of his pain. Then he'd hear her guilt-tripping him, making him feel shitty about what he'd done last night—even though he'd already apologized and she wasn't entirely blameless. If she wasn't so busy keeping an itemized list of his faults maybe she would have more time to be a good wife.

But it wouldn't have mattered, anyway, since she was never home. When Anatoly got off work, she was off helping Americans with their hotel reservations. What did these people need vacations from? They didn't work. But they not only needed vacations—they needed help booking them and needed to go all the way to Ukraine for it. In return, they would offer his wife enough money so that she would think that English was better than Ukrainian and that she was better than her husband, whose salary she didn't even need anymore. When he'd been the one earning the money, she'd often cook him dinner and take care of him. She wasn't fawning or over-the-top—didn't treat him like a child or make him lunch every day like some wives did—but she'd treated his problems like they mattered. Sometimes if he'd had a particularly long day, she'd even bring him a beer and rub his shoulders. Now she was the one who came home to him. He was dreading the night when she'd demand that he rub her shoulders—she'd had such a long day, after all.

His thoughts were making him angrier and angrier, until he had plowed the field down to nothing and then plowed it again, and by then he was so trapped in his anger that he couldn't even make basic decisions. Should he have another cigarette? Should he call his mother? Should he get a coffee on his way home? Should he tell Natalia about the pain? Telling her about his pain would present an opportunity for them to reconcile. But if she rejected his pain, as she almost certainly would, he didn't know what he would do. He was right on the edge. He couldn't take another push. And if she pushed him, he would push back, and then she would make him feel so bad about it that he wouldn't be able to sleep, and then his back would be even stiffer tomorrow. Every scenario he played out just made him angrier until he found it hard to breathe.

But it was a moot point. She would be at her sister's when he got home. She hadn't even said anything to him about his pain, he reminded himself, because he hadn't told her of the pain yet. He'd been infuriating himself with imaginary arguments, sprinkling them with just enough highlights from real arguments to make them feel as if they were actually happening. *What kind of idiot behaved this way? Why get yourself so upset with a drama you've authored, directed, and starred in?* That thought just made him angrier. The car in front of him pulled up short and he almost rear-ended it. He felt his rage bubbling over. He pulled over, got out, and smoked a cigarette. He wanted to hit something and to cry and to make it go away. But his back just hurt so fucking much.

"I don't understand why you have to spend time learning English when you already know English," he'd told her when she'd insisted on resuming her studies with an expensive tutor. "Do you want to go to England or something?"

She looked at him in a way that suggested that he knew the answer to this question. Which he did.

"If you want to go to the Netherlands so badly," he said, "then why don't you learn Dutch?"

"Everyone speaks English in the Netherlands, and there are more international opportunities for English speakers. And where the fuck am I going to learn Dutch?"

"Don't swear at me. I think I'm still your husband."

"You are still my husband. And I love my husband." She came over and put her hand on his chest, lovingly. "But sometimes I wish that he could be open to new things."

"What's wrong with old things?" he said. "What's wrong with our life?" He just wanted things to go back to the way they were.

"Lots of things are wrong with this life."

"You spend four days in Amsterdam with those friends of yours, and now you think you know the place."

"No, I don't think I know it at all! That's why I want to go back!" She sighed in a way that made him furious to remember, even a year later. "But that's not what this is about. I don't care about Amsterdam. We can stay here. What I care about is that I have a great opportunity to make more money at a really interesting job. Don't you want us to have more money? Then we can take a proper holiday. Egypt. Turkey. Cyprus. Some place with lots of sun." She'd embraced him. "Drinking wine on the balcony. Watching the sun set over the sea. You could finally have time to read your philosophy. Wouldn't that be nice?"

Things had been okay for a little bit after that. But they had never taken that vacation. And it had gotten worse when she got the job, a job that they both knew paid far better than his. She hadn't even said, *I told you so*, which meant that the knowledge just hung in the air, unspoken but poisonous, killing any hope at happiness. And then the American had come to town. And moved in right next door! He could kill Bohdan. Years of pretending to be a good neighbor and then he turns the apartment building into a fucking hotel. And then the American banged on his door late at night because he didn't like the way Anatoly was talking to his wife. He would have beaten the shit out of him if Natalia hadn't pleaded with him not to.

And then yesterday, after a grueling shift rolling rocks up a hill to make a better life for his wife, he'd seen the American—this queer who took "little walks" with Natalia every week—prancing about in the courtyard with his headphones in, wearing a fancy coat and fancy shoes like he was the prince of fucking England.

"These Americans," he'd told his wife when he came in. "They come here, they steal our jobs, they steal our women, they throw money around like it's nothing, and then they prance around like queers."

She laughed. "What are you talking about, my dear?"

"You know what I'm talking about. They laugh at our prices and they think they're better than us because they speak English."

"Are you talking about John? You haven't even met him."

"I just saw him prancing around outside. What is he even doing? Did you make dinner?"

"I already ate," she said. "He just likes taking walks. It's harmless. You would understand if you knew him."

"Believe me: I do know him. If you know one, you know them all."

"What other Americans do you know? He's the only American here besides the Jehovah's Witnesses."

"They're Mormons."

She shrugged. "Different God, same idea. There can't be more than ten Americans in Lutsk. What are you complaining about?"

"What's so great about English, anyway? Tell me. It's an idiot's language. *The cat jumped over the fence. The cow lives in the barn.* Anyone can learn it. Does he speak Ukrainian? No. Does he even speak Russian? No." He'd come up the stairs with the idea that he and Natalia would make fun of the American together. That with her on holiday from work, him coming home to her, and the old order restored, they'd be a team again and he would feel better. But now they were opponents and she was on the American's side. He didn't know how this had happened. "He thinks he's better than us because he speaks an easy language. He should try to learn Japanese. Japanese is a difficult language."

"But you don't speak Japanese," Natalia said.

"I'm learning."

"You haven't even opened a Japanese book in years! How are you learning?"

"You know that I have an app on my phone."

Natalia laughed. She fucking laughed at him. "Darling, that app is a game. It doesn't teach you anything."

"When did you decide you were so much better than everyone? Tell me that. When did you decide that you were the boss? When did we all decide that you know better than me and that you were the one who decided in this house and that you were—" Anatoly realized that his wife was making funny sounds. His hands were around her throat. He was squeezing. Her face was red. He felt a sharp pinch in the skin around his wrists. She was grabbing them, trying to get him off. He let go. Backed away. Exhaled.

"I didn't mean to do that. It was a very hard day at work. Darling. I didn't mean to get so excited."

She cried and didn't say anything, even when he apologized.

He did feel bad. Very bad. But he also saw that she was going to milk this one for all it was worth. He went out for an hour to let her cool down. When he came back, she was still sullen, until he told her that they were due for a night out. She didn't act excited, but neither did she protest. She put on a nice dress and heels. When she saw they were going to Show Basilic, she even smiled a little. He ordered champagne and asked her questions to get her to tell her favorite stories. "And Olga! What did Olga say?" When Natalia did a perfect impression of Olga, he banged the table with laughter. And when they got home, he went down on her and didn't even suggest she reciprocate. She went to bed happy. He'd fixed it.

But then in the morning she was cold to him again. She made a point of flaunting the little bruises on her throat, even though he was the one who'd woken up in pain. She'd accepted his apology—an expensive and time-consuming apology—but now she'd decided to revoke it. She wanted to have it both ways!

Looking back on it now, as he walked up the stairs to their apartment, the last stairs of the day, exhausted after a long day's work and with no dinner waiting for him—she wasn't even working this week and she had chosen not to make him dinner after he had spent an arm and a leg on dinner last night—it did bring him some pleasure to remember what he'd done. Sure, he had felt bad about it right afterward. But she had gone out to dinner with him and had a great time, and wasn't that an acknowledgment that he had been right to shut her up? Women will push until you push back; no woman wants a man who doesn't push back. True, he shouldn't have pushed back that hard. Choking wasn't good. He shouldn't do that again. But it would be a moot point if she just stopped pushing.

On the kitchen table, he found a plate of chicken, potatoes, and carrots.

Don't worry, it's not poisoned, said a note by the plate written in Natalia's looping cursive.

A wave of relief. She had forgiven him. And left him food. She was a good wife. He was a lucky man. A lucky man with a good life. He should remind himself of that more often.

He opened a beer and was just sitting down to eat when he heard a knock on the door. Probably the Jehovah's Witnesses again. Who had given them the door code? But when he opened it, he found, confusingly, that the American was standing in the doorway. He wore a blue sweater, a coat too thin to be useful, and jeans that looked expensive and queer. But, despite himself, Anatoly was curious why this man was standing at his door.

"Good evening," the American said in Ukrainian in a high-pitched voice, sounding like a woman.

"Good evening," Anatoly said. "Please." He motioned him inside. He didn't like the American, but he wasn't about to make a guest stand in the hall and let the neighbors think he was some kind of animal.

The American carefully took off his expensive shoes, as if he didn't want them to get dirty in Anatoly's home, then followed Anatoly into the living room. Anatoly didn't know whether to lead him into the kitchen to sit down at the table or to sit down on the couch. He saw the American eyeing their furniture, Natalia's grandparents' furniture that they'd been meaning to replace. Judging it. He even ran a finger over the shelf. Anatoly didn't want to take him into the kitchen to see their ancient refrigerator and the rust that had spread on the washing machine. He wasn't a guest, anyway, but an intruder—what did he want?

The American looked around, uncomfortable, as if not knowing if this was where they were going to talk. *Good. Let him feel uncomfortable.*

"I have a proposition for you," the American said shakily in Ukrainian.

Anatoly had to hold back his smile. The American wanted his help with something. He couldn't wait to tell Natalia. They would laugh at him together.

"Have sex with me," the American said.

It took a minute for the words to register with Anatoly.

"What?" he finally said.

"Have sex with me," the American said. "I will pay you."

"You'll pay me?" Anatoly said. This little queer thought he could come into his house and fuck him? For money?

"Certainly!" the American went on. "Certainly I will pay you. Fifty thousand hryvnias. Yes? But—" He stopped and looked at Anatoly with total contempt. Like Anatoly was some kind of whore. Anatoly reached out and pushed him in the chest, hard, and the American fell back into the shelf and yelped something in English.

"Who do you think I am, you fucking queer," Anatoly said, and charged at him, and the American threw a wild punch, and—

Just then, the wood snapped. His back seized up and something broke in his spine. He screamed. He lurched forward from the pain. The last thing he saw was a fist rising up to meet him.

APRIL 2019

It was shortly after the first round of the Ukrainian presidential election, and directly after the extraction of my wisdom teeth, that I asked Natalia if she wanted to move to America with me.

She tilted her head a little bit, like an infant who's just watched a ball disappear under a couch, and said, "Tell me, what drugs did they give you?"

"I'm serious," I said. She was, technically, correct that I was somewhat-to-extremely high from the laughing gas and anti-anxiety meds the dentist had given me. And the knowledge that I was high had not stopped me from acting high, as I'd imagined it would. But Natalia had been staying over at my place every night for over a month, and I had already told her that I loved her. It wasn't that crazy of a question. "Why not come with me?"

"Because I live here."

"That's true. Right now, we both live here." It was incredibly difficult for me to speak these words, partly because of the gauze jammed into where my teeth used to be and partly because of how distractingly good my socks felt. "But my contract is up at the end of summer. I don't know if it's going to be renewed. And how long do you want to be an agent? I want to plan ahead. With you. We could even go to LA. I would move back there if it meant living with you."

"And what would I do in America?" She was smirking, teasing me, but also stroking my hair.

I was unprepared for this line of questioning. Truth be told, I had no desire to move to America. But I thought that Natalia did, and I wanted to make her happy and start building our life together at the same time. Now that it appeared I'd miscalculated, I knew that there must be an escape route from this conversation—one that didn't signal an approaching expiration date in our relationship. I just couldn't find it. Whether this was due to the drugs or due to my shortcomings as a person, I wasn't sure. But I didn't let it stop me from continuing in the same upbeat tone. "You could do whatever you want in America. Go back to school. Work. Just relax at home. Whatever you want to do, I'll help you."

"This is a very nice idea. But there is the problem of *how*. It's almost impossible for Ukrainians to get tourist visas to *visit* the United States. I don't think I could even get into the country for a holiday. But if I did, how do you think I'm going to just start living there?"

"If we got married you could live there."

She leaned down and looked me in the eyes. She was so beautiful.

"You want to *marry* me?" she said.

"Yeah," I said. And I did. I hadn't thought about it much before that moment—but I did. "Do you want to marry me?"

"Maybe we will discuss this when you are more lucid," she said.

"'Lucid' is a very high-level word," I pointed out, before drifting into half sleep.

Three months had passed since the terrible night with Anatoly. When I'd come back from my alibi-walk and pretended to be arriving on the scene for the first time, Natalia heard me coming up the stairs, rushed past the police, collapsed into my arms, and began to weep. Seeing her exposed and hurt like that was so awful. I was the one who had done it. I was the one who had attacked her husband and likely put him in the hospital. When she sobbed that Anatoly was dead, I thought it must have been shock, confusion. That she'd mixed up her words or forgotten her English. Anatoly couldn't have died from a concussion and a cut on his head.

But as the night wore on and I stayed with her in the apartment while the police milled about, it became undeniable. Anatoly was dead. An officer took Natalia into the living room and another one motioned me into the kitchen. He said something sternly, and I thought the moment had come when I would be arrested. It wasn't fear that hit me but relief. I'd only been living with this secret for a few hours and it already felt like it was enough to break me. I checked my mental storage space to make sure I still had the number to the American Embassy memorized in case they took my phone.

The officer asked me something, and I asked him to please speak slower, as my Ukrainian wasn't very good. The officer asked me if I'd heard any sounds. I tried to explain that I had been out. I mimed walking. The man didn't seem to understand. He returned with another officer who spoke a little English and asked me in English if I'd heard any trouble, fighting, from next door. If I'd seen anyone criminal in the building. I explained that I had been walking home—again, I mimed walking—when the attack had happened. I hadn't seen or heard anything. The officer explained to his colleague. And that was all they asked me.

At the funeral, I watched Anatoly's mother—a short woman in all black who looked like she'd been killed but was still in the process of sending that information from her brain to her body—weeping, screaming. I saw Natalia looking defeated, too tired to cry. I flashed back to taking his wallet. To the way I'd looked around to make sure I was alone before throwing it in the trash can in the park. A spasm of shame shook through me. I waited until I was back in my apartment to cry. I kept crying all day, on and off—every time I thought it was over, it would start again—until I finally fell asleep. Then I woke up and started crying again.

From then on, everything took on a dark tint. As it should have! Guilt, remorse, depression—these were the proper responses to murder. At least it showed I wasn't some kind of psychopath. But I was a murderer. And that wasn't much better.

I took a taxi to Natalia's sister's house outside the city every day, bringing cookies for the children and pizzas for the adults. I thought they thought my behavior strange, but I didn't know what else to do. Natalia and I would sit and talk for a little while every time I visited. None of the looks her relatives gave me suggested that they suspected me of anything more than being a strange foreigner who didn't understand how things were done. But maybe they did; I wouldn't have been able to recognize the look in an unreadable Ukrainian face. Natalia would ask about work and tell me about her nieces. She would try to say funny things about her brother-in-law, but they often got caught in her throat. At some point, every afternoon, she would stop mid-sentence, apparently exhausted from the act of speaking, and excuse herself to go lie down. I kept telling her how sorry I was, without explaining for what, until she told me to stop apologizing.

We didn't talk about Anatoly except for once, briefly. That afternoon, her sister and brother-in-law had taken their children out and the only other person in the house was an older cousin who was watching TV in the other room.

"I'm very angry with him," Natalia said, unprompted. "But I don't think there's anything actionable about my anger."

I told her that this was normal. That anger was a perfectly healthy response. That there were different kinds of grief. I tried to ask her questions to give her a chance to talk more. What was she angry with Anatoly for? How did the anger feel? What was the hardest part about it? But she didn't know. It was too much. I said a bunch of other things that sounded flat and generic even as I was trying to inject them with the feeling I was truly feeling. But I didn't think she heard any of it. Even if I had managed more than just clichés, what could an American teach her about grief?

I couldn't help but think that my dad would've known what to do. How to help. He probably would've said that actions were more helpful than words, so I told Natalia to take all the paid time off she needed and that I would be happy to answer her calls until she returned.

It gave me a good feeling to do something tangible to help Natalia, even if it was so small. But less than halfway through my first shift answering calls, I found, to my surprise, anger bubbling inside me that was difficult to lid. I figured with my experience in food service I would be well equipped for customer support, but almost immediately my patience with the customers began to fray. I wondered if it was displaced anger at myself for what I'd done. I hoped so, as that would be a nobler anger than just being annoyed at aggressive, entitled, perpetually rhetorical-questioning Americans. Within the first hour, two of them asked me, "And you think that's a good way to run a business?"

It was a man from Missouri who broke me. He wanted a cancellation fee waived, as he hadn't realized there was a cancellation fee when he booked the apartment. But more than that, he felt morally offended that we would try to sneak a $100 fee by him.

I explained that, per the agreement the man had signed, there was a fee for any cancellation made more than forty-eight hours after the original booking. The man said that was a ridiculous policy and it was even more ridiculous that we would hide something like that in the fine print.

"I wish I could be of more help, but unfortunately I can't override company policy," I said.

The man reiterated his gripes.

I did not point out that the cancellation fee wasn't, as the man claimed, hidden in the fine print: it was one of only five short bullet points, all in normal-sized font, on the "sign and agree" screen. Instead, I said, "I really am sorry for the inconvenience. It's a very disappointing situation. But when one of our properties is held on a reservation that's later canceled, we lose the opportunity to rent it, and the cancellation fee is in place to indemnify against that eventuality. Unfortunately, since you agreed to the policy, there's nothing I can do."

"That's outrageous," the man said. He told me that he would never be using my company again.

"I'm sorry to hear that. And we're sorry to be losing your business. I wish you had had a better experience with us, but I understand your frustration. I'm also frustrated that I wasn't able to help you."

"I'm sure you are," the man said. He explained that, as soon as he got off the phone, he was going to write a review on every travel site to let customers know what kind of swindlers they'd be working with if they booked with us. If we were worried about losing $100, wait until we saw how much business we were going to lose from his reviews.

And that's when I started to lose it a little bit. "Hold on, sir—I have to alert the others. Guys. Guys. We're about to lose so much business."

The agents looked over at me in confusion.

"Are you kidding me right now?" the man said.

"Absolutely not, sir."

"You know," he said, "I wonder how much needs to go wrong in a man's life before he ends up answering phones for a living."

Luckily, he hung up before I could say anything truly stupid. I was pissed—hopped up on adrenaline and a little blurry. But it was nice to be feeling something different. My brain had been sending signals for days that it wanted to die; now it was screaming that it wanted to survive so that I could defeat this man. Then I felt a light hand on my shoulder. It was Oksana. She waved me out of my seat, motioned for my headset, took my place, and said that she would take over Natalia's calls. Then she sent me home for the day. I didn't think she had the authority to do that, but I did as she said. I felt terrible for failing Natalia, again, and also failing Oksana, and back at home, every time I heard a voice or a clatter from outside I seized up in panic, thinking it was Oksana there to scold me, the police there to arrest me, Natalia there to confront me for what I'd done.

I couldn't sleep, so I came in early the following day, but Oksana was already waiting at my desk to take me to what turned out to be a fairly early lunch. We ate at the same restaurant as the last time and sat at the same table—only I felt like I wasn't at the table at all but was instead watching a grainy videotape of a conversation between an American and a Ukrainian. The two people were talking, mainly the woman, about topics without apparent connection, and then they were eating, and then the woman was telling a story about when she was young and spent an exchange semester in Edinburg, Texas. She'd lived with a family of Ukrainian emigrants while she was there, and early in the morning on her first day, jet-lagged and awake before anyone else, she had walked into the yard to watch the sunrise. She saw with amazement that there were oranges just lying on the ground.

"This was during the hard nineties," she clarified.

Some of the oranges were rotten, but there were several ripe ones, bright and fat, nestled in the grass under their trees. She looked back into the house, pulled her shirt out to make a little basket, and began gathering up the oranges.

"Then, from inside, the mother called my name," she said. "I was so startled that I dropped all the oranges. I was very embarrassed. I thought she would be angry with me for stealing. I began to apologize, to try to explain that I was just bringing them inside so that they didn't spoil. But she said to me, 'No, you must not eat these oranges. They have better oranges at the market.' She ordered me to get dressed and drove us to the store, the biggest supermarket I'd ever seen, and even though it wasn't yet seven in the morning, it was open. She took me to the fruit section, to a mountain of oranges. 'Take,' she said. I took one. 'No,' she said. 'Take as many as you want.' I took two. She grew impatient, opened a plastic bag, and filled it with oranges until she couldn't fit any more in the bag. When we came home, the father wanted to know what they needed so many oranges for. The mother said, 'Oksana wanted them.' I was so ashamed. But the father said, 'Oh, okay.' As if this were a good reason. After that, I ate oranges every day."

When she stopped talking, I came back into myself, realizing the story was over. I wanted to ask if the point of the story was that different people had different standards for what was a good orange—and, by extension, for what was good in general. Or if the story was about wealth—American wealth—and how it distorts your sense of morality to the point where you think it's better to eat oranges from the store than the ones that grow in your own yard. Or if it was some kind of fable to encourage me not to insult the customers.

But at the moment, with my brain fried from anxiety and lack of sleep, trying to articulate any of those things was just too hard. "How did that feel for you?" I said.

Oksana looked confused. Then she shrugged. "So-so."

After lunch, she drove me back to the office without mentioning the call I had screwed up. I got back on the phones that afternoon and handled the rest of Natalia's calls with reasonable competence.

But my days were plagued by increasingly staggering waves of guilt. I began to dread everything, even seeing Natalia, who was the only person I wanted to see. I even toyed with the idea of returning to America simply because it wasn't here. It would be cowardly, immoral, and Western: swoop in, try to be the hero, mess things up for everyone, then get out of town and leave the locals to deal with the consequences. But staying and pretending like I was helping Natalia, like I was this good person, was also immoral. Maybe there was no right thing to do after you'd done something so wrong. What about the least wrong thing to do—what would that be? I was in love with Natalia. But I wasn't helping her. Maybe the only help I could offer her was freedom—not through my presence but through my money. I'd saved up a little over $6,000 from working in Ukraine. I could sneak it through her mail slot and then get out of her life.

Giving her money and leaving her alone started to feel more and more like the right thing to do. But late one night in early February, just as I was resigning myself to the idea, Natalia knocked on my door, suitcase in hand. She said she was moving home from her sister's. But she wasn't ready to go back in the apartment yet.

"Do you want me to come in with you?"

"No." She shook her head. "But maybe you have something to drink?"

I led her into the kitchen, feeling shaky from her presence in my apartment, and apologized for my lack of wine or beer. She said the whisky was fine. We sat in the kitchen with her suitcase by her feet drinking bourbon straight, which she didn't seem to like or not like. She told me about when she first met Anatoly, when she was young, and how everyone had adored him. He was an aspiring journalist. She was studying linguistics. This was at the time of the first revolution, and they were all so full of energy. They would sit up late with their friends and their friends' friends, big groups of ten or twenty people or more—tables spilling over with people—drinking and smoking and arguing. No one ever wanted to go home. There was too much to plan.

"What did you plan?"

"I don't remember. I remember the feeling—but not the plan. Maybe politics, philosophy—the silly things young people get excited about. But when Anatoly was talking, it didn't feel silly. It felt like anything was possible."

We were quiet for a while.

"Why didn't he become a journalist?"

"He did. He was a journalist for some time. But it didn't work."

I told her that I used to be a journalist before I came to Ukraine.

"What happened?" she said.

"It didn't work."

She leaned over and kissed me. Her lips were small and soft and determined. I was burning up with guilt, love, sadness, excitement, regret, desire—too many things at once to make sense—but I kissed her back and found myself in a loop of *oh god this is happening oh god this is happening oh god this is happening oh god this is happening*, and by the time we moved to the bedroom I was so deep in euphoria that I wasn't in my head anymore. I just saw and felt her, and that was all there was in the world.

We didn't say anything afterward. She curled into my body and we fell asleep. I opened my eyes every hour to check, but she was still there. It was the opposite of waking up from a wonderful dream and finding it gone.

In the morning, when it was still dark out, I woke to the sound of her moving. I watched her stand up and take her clothes to the bathroom.

When she returned, I sat up. "How're you doing?" I said.

"I'm doing very well, thank you. How are you doing today, sir?"

I laughed.

"I'm going to go now," she said.

"You can stay."

"No." But before I could feel too bad about it, she came over and kissed me on the cheek, and then on the lips, and said, "Goodbye."

That morning kiss, after a moment of thinking that she was done with me and that it had all been a mistake, felt almost as exciting as the first kiss the night before.

Every day after that was charged with an unbearable excitement at seeing Natalia, alternating with guilt at feeling such excitement. I tried to rationalize it. Anatoly had been an abusive husband. A wife-beater. A man who was terrorizing someone as wonderful as Natalia. I hadn't meant to kill him. But now Natalia was free of him. When I was with her, the rationalization was enough to get me away from the bad thoughts. But when I was alone, I would think, *You are a terrible person.* And then I would think, *But I'm so happy.*

The hours between the early morning, when Natalia snuck back to her apartment so the neighbors wouldn't get any ideas, and late afternoon, when I saw her in the office, were the worst. I lived for the nighttime, when we were alone together. We continued that way for almost a month, until one morning I woke up and the weak sun was shining and she was still there.

"You didn't leave."

"No," she agreed.

"I think I love you," I said, stupidly.

"I understand," she said, and kissed me.

The following weeks were the happiest of my life. My excitement was so constant that even being asleep felt like being awake. One night in March, I got up from bed and went to the kitchen for a glass of water. A snow flurry had covered the streets. The streetlights and the moon reflected off the snow with a brightness that made no sense at night, a brightness that I associated with childhood, even though I'd never woken up to snow as a child. I returned to bed, the room especially dark after the light from the kitchen window, and heard Natalia turning over. I buried my nose in her shoulder blade, put my arm around her stomach, and felt her warm acceptance.

"You are back," Natalia mumbled.

"Yes," I agreed.

"Good."

After a while, feeling awake and alive, I said, "I always wanted to be really good at something."

"What, for instance?" Natalia said softly.

"Didn't really matter. Just to be really good at one thing. Writing. Basketball. Statistics. Something."

"Why?" She ran her fingers over my hand.

"I just like applause, I guess."

"I don't think one receives applause for statistics."

I laughed. "I always thought numbers were fun—the way you could get them to explain things in a way that words can't. I was great at math as a kid—best in my class. 'What's twenty-four times thirteen?' 'Ask John.' 'Three-twelve.' But then they brought in letters, and letters with exponents, and I was lost. I didn't understand calculus. Or even trigonometry, really."

"Maybe basketball is better, then?"

"Maybe."

She kissed my hand.

"When I was young, I wanted to be a dancer," she said.

"Really? What kind?"

"Ballet, of course."

"I could see you as a ballerina."

"I am a ballerina like you are a statistician."

"Why did you stop?"

"I was very good when I was little, like you."

"But then the exponents got you?"

"My feet got me. They grew very big and very flat when I was nine. Before the rest of me grew, my feet were like an elephant."

"Your feet aren't that big."

"Not on an adult! But I've had these feet since I was a child."

I laughed.

"My teacher was furious. 'You think you can dance like this?!' It was like I had made the decision to have enormous flat feet. My mother was so disappointed, too."

"That must have been hard."

"No. To be honest, it wasn't hard. I was getting tired of ballet. So much practice, so much repetition. My toes hurt all the time. My head hurt all the time—they pull your hair up so tight. This way, with my feet getting too big, it was convenient. I didn't even have to quit. And my father was delighted. He wouldn't show it when my mother was around, but when we were alone he gave me books and sweets. 'Well done,' he said. 'Brilliant foot growing. Now we can make puzzles.'"

"He sounds great."

"He was wonderful. I miss him very much."

"I understand," I said. I wanted to tell her about my own father, but it felt like the wrong time. Or maybe I just didn't want to share it—I had so little left of him and I wasn't going to get any more memories. Besides, it didn't feel like we could get any closer than we were in this moment, so I just held her close and was happy.

By April, the happiness had begun to take a physical toll. Or maybe not the happiness so much as the excitement, anxiety, and fear that came with it. My thoughts spiraled out of control at the smallest speed bump, and I startled so easily that every time my phone plinged, the front door clanged downstairs, or there was yelling on the street my body prepared for battle. My teeth and neck and shoulders hurt all the time. I couldn't stop clenching my jaw, which was starting to creak like an old door.

One night, sitting on the couch with Natalia, watching a romantic comedy that she had called touristic, my jaw was hurting so badly that I couldn't stop rubbing it.

"What's wrong?" Natalia said with a note of concern.

"My jaw is just giving me trouble. It's nothing new."

"Have you been to a doctor?"

"It's just stress. Sometimes it feels like my teeth don't fit in my mouth."

"Maybe you need to have some teeth out."

"I meant figuratively."

"Yes, I meant actually," she said.

The next day, the dentist confirmed that I needed to have some teeth out.

"Your wisdom teeth are infected," Natalia translated as I sat in the chair.

"But they were always fine. You're not supposed to have problems with your wisdom teeth in your thirties."

She translated for the dentist, and the dentist shrugged his shoulders wordlessly. "He says that maybe it is because you are so wise," Natalia said.

"I don't think that's what he said."

The doctor said something else.

"So," Natalia said, "he'll take them out?"

"I guess. When does he want to do it?"

"*Zaraz*," the dentist had said. Now. The way he'd said it implied that of course he would take them out now—when else would he take them out?

I only remembered bits and pieces of the operation: feeling like the laughing gas mask was slipping off but never falling, a nurse holding my head, the sound of the crunch when the dentist pulled the teeth out, and a feeling of painless well-being. I remembered afterward, asking Natalia to marry me. I did not remember getting an answer. But in the morning, she changed my bloody gauze and helped fill in some of the gaps in my memory. Apparently, after the procedure, I'd insisted that she translate several jokes for the dentist.

"Did he think it was funny?"

"It may have lost something in the translation."

"Did you think it was funny?"

"Very funny," she said, and wedged a lump of gauze into the cavern behind my top right molar.

"What happened next?"

She said that she had called Dima to come pick us up, since she didn't want to take me on a bus or a taxi, and, apparently, I had walked to the car "with the confidence of a much faster man."

"Dima was there?"

"Yes, he drove us home and you two had a very long conversation about the future of commerce."

I had said the globalized economy was going to create great opportunities that were going to change the lives of all Ukrainians.

"Dima also believed this to be true," Natalia said. "But he was not on drugs, so I don't know why."

Then I had slept for a while, but Dima had insisted on staying and making me food. According to Natalia, Dima said that I needed pork and potatoes to make me strong. Natalia explained that I could not eat potatoes and pork because of the large wounds in my mouth. So Dima boiled pork and potatoes together into a soup.

"It was pink and vile. But you ate two bowls and insisted that

Dima should sell it on Amazon, and then you fell asleep, and later you woke up screaming, and I was worried that you had been poisoned. But then we talked some and you fell back to sleep, and now it's now, so it appears Dima's cooking did not kill you."

I had been screaming because Anatoly, blissfully absent from my thoughts for weeks, had come storming back on a cloud of medicated sleep. I couldn't remember exactly what he'd said or done—but I remembered the dread that came from his presence. The dread was much worse because I couldn't talk to Natalia about it—it was something between us now that we couldn't break down together. But it was still comforting to have her there, telling me what happened. She was so certain about everything, so unlike my own memory when I replayed events, that it wiped away all the anxiety.

"Thank you," I said.

"For what?"

"For taking care of me."

She looked annoyed. "Please."

"I think I asked you to marry me. But I'm not sure if that was a dream."

"It was real," she said. "But we don't need to discuss this currently."

Then she wrapped me up in her arms and I fell asleep.

Among the many things that I apparently said in the aftermath of my surgery, one was that Dima should come over to watch the presidential debate that Friday. He showed up at my apartment in the early evening of a pleasant spring day with a bottle of wine in hand.

"To be honest, John, I don't know anything about wine," he said. "But the girl said this one was good."

Natalia was in the kitchen when he arrived and didn't come out to greet Dima, but if he registered anything odd about that, he didn't show it.

"This will be great," Dima said, motioning to the pre-debate commentary on the TV.

I felt the same way. I was excited about watching history in the making. Also, a little high on painkillers.

This hadn't been expected to be an exciting election. A contest between the same old oligarchs had been looming like a dentist's appointment. But then, on New Year's Eve, a new figure announced his candidacy: the actor Volodymyr Zelensky. Zelensky played the president of Ukraine on the popular TV show *Servant of the People*, which I sometimes thought taught me more about Ukraine than my limited-to-mostly-English-language life did. In the show, Zelensky—

a short, dark-haired man with a deep voice—played a schoolteacher who's unexpectedly elected president of Ukraine. It is a comedy of errors and sincerity, as the schoolteacher learns how to be president—one of the first lessons he gets is how to ask the United States for money—while fighting corruption and oligarchy. In the first round of the real presidential election, Zelensky had smashed the competition, and now he would face off against the incumbent, Poroshenko, in a runoff.

It had occurred to me, even before the influx of opiates made anything seem possible, that if I wanted to dip my toes back into American journalism, I was in a great position to cover this important Ukrainian election from the ground. I'd sketched out some notes and had even attended a political speech by the third-place candidate in the town square. But over the past few weeks, I had so fully enjoyed the imaginary spoils of writing my article—the praise from the editor, the social media applause, the handshakes from the developers in my office for being one of the few Western journalists to cover Ukraine in an honest and respectful manner—that I didn't feel motivated to pursue it further.

The TV cut to the soccer stadium where the debate was set to kick off. It was not normal for Ukrainian political debates to be held in sports stadiums, but the unusual setting, as far as I could follow, had come about because the incumbent, Poroshenko, trailing in the polls, was eager to debate the actor, Zelensky, in order to expose the actor's lack of a political position. Zelensky was less eager to debate, since a big part of his appeal was that he hadn't said very much and voters could project their hopes onto him and see him as his character on TV, a unifier who fought corruption, rather than as a real person. But Zelensky finally agreed to debate Poroshenko, on the condition that the debate not take place in some TV studio. Zelensky would only participate if the debate was held in the national soccer stadium—so that the people could attend! Zelensky did sometimes sound like his American showman-politician counterpart in their appeals to populism, but he and the American president enjoyed support from the exact opposite bases. Large crowds came to see the American president tell them who to blame; Zelensky's crowds wanted a way forward for all Ukrainians, regardless of where they lived or what language they spoke.

Dima and Natalia sat on either side of me on the couch, Natalia and I with wine, and abstinent-for-one-year Dima with a glass of juice, and we watched the camera pan around the soccer stadium. It was a strange setup. Each candidate had their own stage, at either end of the field, so that the candidates were facing each other, but over one hundred yards away. Zelensky looked hip and slick, Poroshenko large and battle-tested. Both of them had massive entourages filling their stage. There were maybe twenty thousand spectators, many of them standing on the field, like at a rock concert for an aging band that was trying to squeeze out one last farewell tour.

Zelensky opened by saying something to Poroshenko. The crowd cheered. Then, at the other end of the field, Poroshenko left his stage to the roar of the crowd. Followed by his entourage, he walked the running track that circled the soccer field toward Zelensky's stage.

"What's happening?" I said.

"Poroshenko is walking," Natalia said, monotone. "The crowd is very happy about this."

"Zelensky has challenged Poroshenko to join him on a single stage," Dima said. "Poroshenko has accepted." He paused. "Poroshenko is not very fast."

After some scrambling, a second mic was set up. Both entourages squeezed behind the candidates onto a now-very-crowded stage. Natalia groaned and went to the kitchen. She returned a few minutes later with a bottle of *horilka,* Ukrainian vodka, glasses, and a bowl of potato chips.

Zelensky was saying something and his supporters were going nuts; I could only make out the words for "Ukraine," "Russia," and "people."

"What's he saying?"

"He is saying," Natalia said, "in Russian, that it's okay to speak Russian."

Dima clarified that this was not precisely what he was saying. The crowd was excited that Zelensky had broken into Russian for a few sentences.

"He said that those who died on the Maidan spoke Russian," Dima said. "And I think it's good for him to say this."

All political proceedings, by law, were conducted in Ukrainian. But there were more Ukrainians who spoke Russian as their first language than Ukrainian, in large part due to the legacy of Soviet restrictions of the Ukrainian language. The speaking of Russian did not necessarily mean that a person was pro-Russia. But during the 2014 revolution, the Ukrainian language had become a crucial piece of Ukrainian independence. Poroshenko, who was a native Russian speaker, only spoke Ukrainian in public, and made the championing of the Ukrainian language a central part of his platform. Russia used this favoring of the Ukrainian language to spread propaganda. The Russian disinformation division, the greatest disinformation machine in the world, had long used Ukraine as their testing ground. They circulated videos on YouTube falsely claiming that the Ukrainian government was persecuting and murdering Russian speakers, and these videos were recirculated by real Ukrainians and Russians who believed them to be true. Russian operatives rented the social media accounts of real Ukrainians for several hundred dollars per month to spread propaganda so that it could be seen as coming from your coworker or uncle instead of just fake accounts and bots. The mostly imagined persecution of Russian speakers in Ukraine was supposed to justify the need for Russian military intervention in Ukraine—even though Russia denied intervening.

By speaking Russian while also condemning Russia, Zelensky was pleading for nuance. He was arguing that a Ukrainian could be a patriot and a Russian speaker at the same time. But I might just have been mirroring my own feelings onto him.

"I read an article," I said, "that said sixty percent of Ukrainians believe this election will be rigged."

"Rigged?" Dima said.

I explained what the word meant.

"But the article also said that eighty percent of Ukrainians plan to vote anyway," I said. "That means, if my math is correct, that at least half the people who plan to vote believe that the election will not be fair. But they're still going to vote." It could have been the general good vibes I was experiencing wedged between the girl I loved and my best friend in Ukraine, but I found the notion of choosing to vote in a rigged election to be moving. "I find that notion moving."

Apathy was the goal of Russian interference—getting a populace so confused and exhausted by lies that they stop listening, stop caring, stop participating in democracy. It was so easy to succumb to cynicism. But Ukrainians were saying, *Fuck you. I'm voting anyway.*

"Do you think it will be rigged?" I asked Natalia.

"Probably, yes."

"Are you going to vote?"

"Of course."

"Why?"

She shrugged. “Why not?”

“Are you going to vote?” I said to Dima.

“Yes, I am very excited. This will be the first time I vote.”

“Who are you going to vote for?”

“Zelensky, of course.”

I tried to follow a point Poroshenko was making about the military and Putin, but I got lost and found my thoughts drifting to the American media’s coverage of Ukraine over the last few weeks. American journalists had been concerned about the rise of Zelensky in ways that at times it seemed like worry-trolling or explicit condescension. An actor! With no political experience! Going toe-to-toe with Putin! They were so alarmed that any country would make such a decision.

I had doubts about Zelensky. I wasn’t sure what to believe about him. But he wasn’t an oligarch. Nor did he seem to be a dangerous sower of fear and division, like the last showman politician I’d seen. If anything, his message seemed to be unity. He at least had the chance of not being corrupt. If I was Ukrainian, I would vote for him.

The debate turned to oligarchs, the people who, in the aftermath of the fall of the Soviet Union, had hoarded vast wealth, often through criminal means. For Ukraine, this was a group of about fifty people who, for years, controlled over 80 percent of the country’s wealth. The number had shrunk some since the revolution, but it was still a country ruled by oligarchy. Poroshenko said something about oligarchs. Then Zelensky said something else about oligarchs and the crowd went wild.

“Poroshenko accused Zelensky of being under the control of an oligarch,” Dima explained. “Because the man who owns the television station that broadcasts Zelensky’s program is an oligarch, and this man is also a friend of Zelensky’s. So Poroshenko is saying that Zelensky will be influenced by this oligarch. Then Zelensky answered, ‘But, Poroshenko, you *are* an oligarch!’”

"That's a good comeback."

"Yes, I thought it was very clever. And true. Poroshenko is one of the richest men in Ukraine."

The more the debate went on, the more my attention waned. A soldier standing behind the president answered his phone while the president was talking. I thought this the most Ukrainian thing about the whole night: there was never a time when it was unacceptable to answer your phone. I tried to stop my thoughts from drifting back to Anatoly, who had been visiting my dreams every night since the surgery. I'd tried to sleep without the pain pills that were causing the nightmares, but the throbbing in my jaw was too strong.

"This is a fiasco," Natalia said, bringing me back from the unpleasant thoughts.

The candidates were walking offstage.

"It wasn't perfect," Dima said. "But it's not impossible to have something that isn't perfect still be good. I'm excited for Zelensky."

"Why?" Natalia said. "He will just be like all the rest."

"Natalia, Ukraine is like a girl," Dima said. "She—"

"No no no," Natalia said. "If I have to hear 'Ukraine is like a girl' one more time, I'm going to hit someone."

"Pardon me," Dima said. "Ukraine is like a *woman*." One day, I had explained to the agents why you couldn't call an adult woman a "girl" or an adult man a "boy" in English like you did in Ukrainian, and for reasons I would probably never understand since I'd never be a native speaker of Ukrainian, Dima found this linguistic difference very funny.

Natalia hit him in the shoulder; I laughed.

I asked Dima to explain how Ukraine was like a woman.

Natalia said she couldn't listen to any more of this nonsense and started gathering glasses from the table.

Dima implored her to wait, then said something in Ukrainian. She groaned and sat back down. "Ukraine is like a woman," he went on. "She is beautiful. She is delicate."

"She has a gas problem," Natalia added.

"She is tough," Dima continued. "She perseveres. She will not perish. But she has been mistreated for a very long time. And there is only so long that a woman can be mistreated before she breaks. To be honest, I thought that Maidan was the break. But maybe this is the real break, this election. Not with violence or revolution—but with intellect. With emotion. A woman's solution. If Ukraine is like a woman, maybe she needs a woman's solution."

Everyone was quiet for a minute.

"Dima is like a woman," Natalia said, and went to the kitchen.

"How am I like a woman?" Dima yelled after her. "How am I like a woman? Tell me, John, how am I like a woman?"

But I was laughing too hard to answer.

The morning after the election was an exciting one. As it turned out, the election was not rigged. It was one of the most closely watched elections in modern history, with countless international and domestic observers present—yet no major irregularities were reported. Even the loser said that it had been fair. Zelensky won in a landslide with 73 percent of the vote. It was a historic day for Ukraine: a new president, a transfer of power, and an election fairly held with no bloodshed. But even with the historic day for Ukraine, I was equally, if not more, excited about waking up without pain. My jaw had finally stopped throbbing, which meant I could stop taking the pills. Last night, as I slept, Anatoly sat down at my childhood kitchen table, dressed in a red cardigan, and began reading the *LA Times*. The night before, he and I had played catch on a beach at sunset. With each dream, his existence grew, and then I would remember that I had ended it, and everything from that night would come back again in all its terribleness. Now that the pain was finally gone, I could stop taking the pills, banish him from my mind, and return to the present.

But I noticed, upon my return to the present, that Natalia seemed a little distant. I couldn't tell if she'd been this way all week and I'd failed to notice, or if it was something new. When we had sex that morning, it felt like she was elsewhere. Even when she was coming it felt like she was elsewhere. I tried to ask her about it, but either she didn't want to talk or I was asking in the wrong way. It didn't bother me the way it normally would, though. I felt confident that once Anatoly was gone from my consciousness, things would go back to the way they had been.

At the office, everyone was talking about the election. One of the older developers said that he had voted for the incumbent. The president, Poroshenko, had many problems, he said. But for all those problems, he was still a Ukrainian patriot pushing the country to Europe and the EU. He was stable, and most importantly, he was a known quantity.

"We don't know anything about Zelensky," the developer said. "But I don't know. Maybe Zelensky will be better."

Kyle, who was probably the youngest in the office, wasn't as exuberant as I expected. He said he had voted for Zelensky. "But still, I wonder, maybe, did I make the right decision? I don't know."

Oksana didn't know either. She said that maybe a change was necessary.

"Our education system is bad, healthcare is bad, and people are dying younger than in the past from low pensions. The population is shrinking. Things are getting better. But slowly. Unless you can start your own business, it's better to leave to work elsewhere. A woman who is a teacher in Ukraine can go to Europe and be a nurse for an old person and make five times the salary she makes here. I don't know if Zelensky will fix this. Maybe."

Ukrainians seemed to have a lot more doubt in the aftermath of an election than Americans. The day after an American election, I was sure that either the right candidate had won, the wrong candidate had won, or the whole system was broken. *I don't know, maybe?* seemed to be the dominant Ukrainian reaction.

The only person who seemed unabashedly happy was Dima.

"Zelensky is the future!" he said. "A young guy, not a politician, not an oligarch. And seventy-three percent vote for him! Can you believe this? As a Ukrainian, I've always dreamt of this."

I wanted to hear more of Dima's optimism—this was exactly the type of joy I'd been looking for—but just as he suggested we head upstairs for a coffee, my phone buzzed. Davey.

I excused myself into the stairwell to take the call. After his pep talk in January, he'd texted a few times with an encouraging note or just to check in. But we hadn't talked in at least a month, and he had yet to respond to my last email outlining a plan for how to train the agents to take on chat tickets.

"Hey, Turner, am I interrupting?" Davey said, which didn't sound like him at all.

"Not at all! Good to hear from you, my guy."

"How're things on your side of the pond?"

"Oh, they're great. It's an exciting time here."

"Glad to hear it," he said. He was silent after that.

"Did you read the report I sent?" I said. "Now that we've cut average call times to nine minutes, I think that we could use some of what we've learned to optimize chat—"

"That's actually what I wanted to talk to you about. I've found a really great opportunity to right-source our customer support."

Davey explained that he'd been in talks with an agency based in a small town in Oregon that offered bespoke support services tailor-made to the client. They were going to take over all support duties.

"What do you mean?"

He said that I had done a great job with the team in Ukraine—better than could be expected. But the thing was, we had a chance to maximize our quality in a really exciting way here.

"With the new team," he said, "we'd have a dedicated squad of five agents with customer support experience who go through a support boot camp to learn specifically about *our* company. Then those agents work exclusively with us to custom-tailor the support experience as we expand our presence."

"But that's what we're doing here," I said, catching my voice getting louder. I quieted down, made sure no one else was in the hallway, and repeated in a calmer voice, "That is literally exactly what we're doing here."

"Well, not exactly." He explained that in the Oregon office we'd have American agents. They wouldn't have to be trained to sound American.

I trembled, found it hard to breathe. I had already decided to stay in Lutsk. My contract—or "agreement," since we hadn't actually signed anything—was up in September, but things had been going so well that it hadn't occurred to me that Davey might not want to renew. I was meeting the quotas he'd set. The agents were getting better every day. And now he wanted to end it?

"But what about the smart-sourcing philosophy that's the foundation for the whole venture? Hiring American agents is going to cost you so much more money."

Davey said that, actually, that wasn't the case. If we were hiring agents in the Bay Area or Seattle, sure, that would be true. But in small towns in Oregon, you could hire good agents for fifteen dollars an hour.

I pointed out that fifteen dollars per hour was still ten dollars more per agent per hour than he was paying our agents. "With five agents, you'd be increasing your support costs one hundred thousand dollars per year. Even if the American agents sound a little more natural, that's a big number for a marginal improvement. Is that a good way to run a business?"

Davey said that, actually, with the numbers we were seeing, $100,000 wasn't that much money. His speech slowed down, like he was reading an email on a different screen. "Look, I know this is a surprise. But don't worry—I'm not hanging you out to dry. I'm still going to honor our deal. You'll be paid in full through the summer."

"But, my guy, this is not smart. You've already put all the time and money into training five good agents. And now that they're hitting their stride, you're going to let them go instead of utilizing the money you've put into them?" I tried to remember which sport was Davey's favorite. "It'd be like spending years nurturing a draft pick in the minors and then when he's ready for the show trading him away for nothing."

"Sunk costs, Turner. You can't make decisions based on sunk costs."

"But what about the office?"

"We'll still use it for the developers. It'll just revert to its original purpose."

"Is this because of the election? Because I think the foreign press is being really alarmist."

"What election?"

I sighed. "We can turn this around. Just tell me what you need. I'll deliver. I guarantee it. If you don't see the results you want by the end of next month, we'll terminate the whole operation—no argument. You don't even have to pay me out."

"Turner, it's done. I signed the papers last week."

I rubbed my eyes. I imagined having to tell the agents. Having to tell Natalia. "When are you shutting us down?"

"End of the week."

"This week?"

"Correct."

"You can't be serious."

"These things move quickly."

"Are you paying out the agents, too?"

"What do you mean?"

"Are you giving them severance?"

"They're hourly."

I heard a door open, and a man from the upstairs office trotted down the stairs. I waited until he left.

"I should've known," I said. "You always do this."

"Do what?"

"Lose interest. Leave the old toy as soon as you get a new one. This is just like college."

"I'm not losing interest—I'm growing my company. Growing my business. That I started. That I, alone, am responsible for. You have no idea what that's like. Tough decisions have to be made. My responsibility is not to the agents, or the developers, or to you—it's to the shareholders."

"You don't even have shareholders!"

"But I'm going to. And once we go public, how's it going to look to have a call center in the country with the second-lowest EPI score in Europe?"

"What the fuck is an EPI score?"

"I don't know, man, it measures, like, how good you are at English."

I took a breath. "Look, just tell me this. Are customers satisfied with my agents?"

"They are." He paused. "And they aren't."

"What do you mean? What are they doing wrong?"

He sighed. "The most common complaint is that they sound Russian."

With that, I felt myself give up. Davey softened his tone and said that he appreciated how much I cared but that it was time to move on. He promised that he'd try to hook me up when I got back to the States.

After I hung up, I felt like the room was on fire. But when I imagined escaping, I realized it wasn't possible because I was the room. I leaned against the wall outside the office and tried to gather myself. When I heard Dima and the others returning from a coffee break, I hurried back inside. I sat down at my desk and pretended to answer emails. While the agents took calls and the developers headed home for the day, I sat at my desk replaying the conversation, trying to think of something I could have done differently, or something I could still do differently to change Davey's mind. But I kept coming back to the same fact: the Ukrainians could get a hundred times better at attentive listening, American diction, questions instead of commands, and small talk, but they would still "sound Russian."

In the past, I would've fantasized about beating the shit out of Davey—would've imagined it so viscerally that I would have forgotten where I was until I opened my eyes to the room in front of me and found my teeth clenched together and my heart pumping. But I couldn't even indulge that fantasy anymore, for obvious reasons. Instead, I found myself imagining Davey giving me a hug and telling me it was okay. He'd changed his mind. Of course he'd keep the office open. God. How pathetic.

I watched the agents on their headsets. Andy said to a customer, "Very good, sir. Let's see if we can't fix this problem." He was getting so much better. He and Kyle were young and still lived with their parents—they'd be okay. Oksana had two other jobs. But Lisa and Angie had children. "I am jealous!" Angie said to a customer with the perfect light tone. "I have never been to Miami. You'll have to have a cocktail by the pool for me. Yes? . . . Okay, thank you very much." What would happen to their families next week, when they lost their income?

I went to their Facebook pages to try to learn what their husbands did for a living, but the only recent post I found was a picture of Angie posing in front of a new black Škoda. She looked so happy. It was not like her other posed pictures with the perfect lighting: this one had an unguarded smile, like her husband had snapped a photo at the exact moment she'd realized she finally made it. What if they lost that car? What if she lost her house? And what would happen with Natalia? I couldn't even begin to think of that. I decided right then to split my severance with the agents; there was no reason I should be the only one getting paid to do nothing.

Late into the evening, I searched job listings on the Ukrainian sites I knew, then tried to find more sites. But it was obvious that there were no other prospects for me in Lutsk. The image of Anatoly flashed before me, sitting at the kitchen table dressed in that red cardigan. The memory of that cardigan, which I'd never actually seen him wear, was so haunting. I squeezed my eyes shut and tried to return to the moment—the meager Ukrainian job postings on the screen. Even if I found a job teaching English, no easy task, the pay would be a Ukrainian salary—so little so as to not make it worth it. Plus, I was in the country illegally, which would certainly complicate the job search.

But I couldn't leave. I couldn't lose Natalia. And I didn't want to go home. It was only once I got out of the United States that I realized how tiring it had become to live there. I had tried to disengage from politics back home, as much as such a thing was possible, to get away from the doomy hopelessness of Trump's America. But even if I'd been able to block out the noise at work and with my friends, my dad wouldn't let me. Since the 2016 election, he'd wanted to talk about nothing but the hateful man in the White House—which had surprised me, since my dad was normally pretty uninterested in politics. But now he sent me articles I didn't want to read several times a week and started almost every phone call with, "Did you see what old Donny did today?" He told me over and over that this man was the greatest threat to American democracy he'd ever seen. I agreed with him. I hated the president, too. I had even marched against him—only once, granted, but that was once more than I'd ever marched against anything else. I just couldn't talk about it all the time. If I was going to survive these years without falling into total despair, I couldn't worry and fret about every single thing he said and did. It was why I'd been dodging my dad's calls. It was why I hadn't picked up the last time he'd called. I didn't want to go back to all that.

Through the rest of my shift, I thought about what I would say to Natalia. How to break the news to her and how to convince her that we should stay together anyway. I got home a little before her, changed into my best casual button-up, made us an omelet, and opened a bottle of chilled white wine. She was in a good mood, and over dinner she told a funny story about her brother-in-law—how Oleksander now had plans to design an app, even though he was an administrative bureaucrat with no technical expertise. All he needed was a computer guy.

"So he's going to do it with his brother's son," Natalia said, "who's really good with computers."

"How old is the son?"

"Nine!"

I laughed. It didn't feel mean to laugh at Oleksander. When I'd met him after Anatoly's death, he seemed like kind of a dick and always talked over women.

Our laughter died down, Natalia kissed me, and I kissed her back, and it felt like she was present again. Only now I was elsewhere. She moved her hand down to my belt, but I stopped her.

"I have to tell you something."

"You are pregnant," she said.

I smiled.

"Oh. Something serious." She got up and poured another glass of wine. "I understand. Tell me, please."

"I talked to Davey today." I told her everything. I told her Friday would be our last day. I told her it was a stupid, impulsive decision by a stupid, impulsive person. I told her that I had tried to talk him out of it but that he wouldn't budge. I told her I was still trying to think of ways to change his mind. "But he's already signed the papers. I'm so sorry."

Natalia thought it over for a minute. "Why are you sorry? It's not your decision."

"I feel like I could have done more."

She shrugged, as if to say, *Okay.*

"He's going to pay me through the end of the summer. But he's not going to pay you or the other agents."

"That's good, John."

"It's not good. It's terrible."

"You are being dramatic."

I took a breath and explained my plan. Over the next four months, I was going to be paid $12,000 to do nothing. I planned to give half my severance to the agents who got laid off and take the other half to move somewhere. We could get married and live in any city she wanted. The Republic of Georgia had a deal with the United States that made it easy for Americans to get residency permits, and as my wife it would be easier for her, too. We could live in Tbilisi. Or we could go to the Continent. Lisbon, Florence, Madrid. Anywhere she wanted.

"This is foolish."

"It's not foolish," I said. I felt Anatoly in his cardigan trying to squeeze between us; I tried to push him away. "It's an opportunity."

"Please, John." She sat back down at the table. "This news, with Davey, this is not a catastrophe. It's just a thing that happened. It doesn't have to change the whole world."

"But what will you do?"

"I'll find another job."

"Doing what?"

"I don't know. Maybe more customer support. Maybe I'll become a tour guide. More and more Europeans are coming to Lviv, and I know that city well. Or maybe I'll help Oleksander with his app. There are many possibilities."

"Be serious."

"I am serious. I've had jobs before this one. I can find another one."

"What about Amsterdam? We could move there."

She put her glass down and placed her hand on mine. "I will find another job here. You will go back to America. You will use your money to start your new life. You will not give it to the agents. They don't need your charity. You cannot solve everything by paying people."

I flinched at those words. But they didn't seem to carry any extra significance to her.

"With that much money," she continued, "you can do whatever you want. Maybe you can start your own magazine. You could be a journalist again." She paused. She opened her mouth to speak but exhaled instead. I couldn't tell if she was overcome by emotion or struggling to find the English words.

"But I love you," I said.

"I love you, too.. Isn't that wonderful?" She was crying now. She took my face between her hands. "Why destroy it? Why not just leave it wonderful?"

To announce the closure to the office, I recited a statement that I'd memorized ahead of time to make sure I didn't let my emotions get in the way of communicating how I actually felt. I told the agents, sitting at their desks and looking up at me with blank expressions much like they had on my first day, how proud I was of them and how none of this was their fault. But after I delivered the bad news, everyone stayed quiet.

"Yes, we know," Kyle finally said.

I looked at Natalia. She looked away.

"I want you to know that this has nothing to do with your performance. You've all done an exceptional job. I don't agree with this decision. I don't agree with it at all."

The agents didn't say anything. I didn't know what to say.

Finally, Natalia said, "Thank you, John. We are appreciative."

The agents nodded.

It would have been inappropriate to cry—you don't cry when you're hurting someone else; you don't force them to comfort you and deprive them of the anger they should rightly be directing at you—but I certainly wanted to.

"Okay," Oksana said. "We will open the lines now."

Everyone started working as if nothing had changed.

Natalia and I talked about it at home. She reassured me and was kind, which felt backwards. I didn't bring up the future. I tried to keep it wonderful and hoped that maybe she would change her mind. But even without the pills, Anatoly kept visiting me at night. It was hard to picture a bright future with him in it.

The last night at the office, after we closed the lines, we had a little party in the banquet hall downstairs. I gave 10,000 hryvnias, about $400, to each of the agents. It was not nearly the "charity" sum that Natalia had cautioned me against giving away, but it was two weeks' severance pay—the least that they were entitled to. To my surprise, when I began handing the envelopes out at the party I found that they all had gifts for me. Angie gave me a box of Irish cream shooter chocolates. Andy gave me a Ukrainian national team soccer jersey. Kyle gave me a bottle of *horilka*. Oksana gave me a bottle of cognac. Lisa gave me a puzzle of a map of Ukraine. Natalia gave me a leather-bound journal. This time I couldn't hold back the tears. But it was three in the morning, and with alcohol and sentiment flowing it seemed like an acceptable time to cry. Andy and Lisa cried, too. We hugged and danced, and they all taught me Ukrainian songs and I joyously mumble-sang along with them. At dawn, we hugged our goodbyes and agreed to stay in touch via a Facebook group that Kyle was going to start.

When I woke around noon to the smell of the coffee Natalia was making, wretchedly hungover, I picked up my phone and found the invite from Kyle. *You are invited to join the group: BULLETPROOF.*

I HADN'T INTENDED TO WATCH THE HBO MINISERIES ABOUT Chernobyl, as I'd always avoided watching movies or shows that I knew would end in disaster. What was the point in spending that much time dreading the ending you knew was coming? But Dima invited me over to his place to watch the first three episodes, which he had illegally downloaded, and even though we'd only been shut down for a little over a week, I missed seeing him at the office every day. When I showed up, Natalia and Oksana were already there, and I soon found myself sitting with old colleagues who didn't seem to resent me, drinking wine, eating salami and cheese, and watching what was turning out to be a spellbinding show.

I thought I knew how Chernobyl ended, but apparently all I knew was the beginning: the reactor exploded. After the explosion, there was the race to control the burn, limit the damage, evacuate the area, save as many people as possible, and, most of all, convince the Party bosses of the severity of the problem. On numerous occasions during the first episode, I found myself holding my breath. Oksana and Natalia were quiet, looking equally caught up in the action. Dima was the only one talking. He couldn't stop yelling at the Party bureaucrats who kept denying the crisis—costing countless lives in the process—because they didn't want to admit to their superiors that there was a problem.

"My parents, they say everything was better during communism," Dima said. "But they just think it was better because that's when they were young. Look at who was in charge. These were the people who ruled the country! It's the core that's exploded, not the tank, idiot!"

Besides the fact that all the actors appeared to be British or Scandinavian, the portrayal of 1980s Ukraine felt realistic to me—or it at least felt true to what I had experienced of 2010s Ukraine: the buildings, interactions, social norms, and mood. Which suggested either that Ukraine had not changed much over the last three decades or that both 1980s and 2010s Ukraine were so different from anything I had previously experienced that, next to each other, they looked nearly the same.

"Oksana, does it feel realistic to you?" I said, since Oksana was the only one who was old enough to remember the eighties and she also gave Chernobyl tours on the side.

"Yes," she said.

I looked at Natalia for confirmation that this was strange—Oksana passing up the chance to speak. But Natalia's attention was on the show.

On-screen, a Belarusian scientist went to her Party leader to warn him that the officials on the ground were wrong and that devastation was on the horizon. But the Party leader was a fat, arrogant idiot—a man who knew better than scientists, even if he knew nothing of science. This led Dima into a rant about the idiocy of a system that makes uneducated idiots get to decide science over scientists.

"What do you think, Oksana?" I said. "You remember both. Was it better during communism? Or now?"

"It was bad then," Oksana said, staring at the screen. "And good." She shrugged without looking away from the action. "Different."

I was starting to get a little tipsy from the wine. The wife of a firefighter who was dying from radiation exposure had snuck into his hospital room. The firefighter's wife wanted to be there with him for his last hours, despite his radioactivity, which was so strong that each second next to him reduced her life expectancy measurably. I reached out to squeeze Natalia's hand. She distractedly squeezed it back, then let go.

After the last episode ended, Oksana broke her silence. "John, do you think this show will be popular in America?"

"I think so. It's gotten very good reviews already."

Oksana started to say something else, but Dima interrupted. "Do you think Americans will be more interested in Ukraine as a result?"

Oksana said something to Natalia in Ukrainian. The two of them picked up the snack dishes and the empty bottles and disappeared into the kitchen.

"Could it be a marketing opportunity?" Dima said.

I confessed that I wasn't sure that there was much opportunity for capitalizing on the popularity of a miniseries via earplugs.

"This is good to know," Dima said. "It's fortunate that I have you as a friend."

I felt myself blush at the word "friend."

Back at my apartment, Natalia and I opened a bottle of wine. We sat in the kitchen and talked about the show and laughed about Dima's relentless energy. But it felt like Natalia's thoughts were divided.

"What are you thinking about?"

"I'm thinking about when you'll return to America," she finally said. "I'm both anxious for you to go and not wanting you to go, if that makes sense."

"Then I'll stay."

"That wasn't what I meant."

"I know." My mouth felt dry from the wine. I ran my tongue

over the roof of my mouth and swallowed. "I understand that your life is here. I'm not ignorant of that." I took a breath. "I hope you know that I wasn't asking you to move away with me as some kind of fantasy—some dream that I'm going to get bored with once it becomes real. I know what a serious thing I was asking of you. I realize now that I made a mistake in treating it like it wasn't a big deal. I'm sorry." I paused.

"With the way you talked about Holland, or the way Dima talks about America, or even the way people here talk about Poland like it's the center of the world, I thought you wanted something more. But I misunderstood. I thought you had to go abroad to get something more. But now I understand: You don't have to leave Ukraine. You can have it here. *We* can have it here."

I felt her softening, like I'd finally found the right track. I put my hand on hers and saw our life in Ukraine stretching out before us. We didn't have to leave Ukraine—we just had to leave Lutsk. Leave this apartment. Leave Anatoly. "What if we moved to Lviv?" I said. "You can be a tour guide, like you said. You can start your own company. And I can be a journalist again. Ukraine is an important part of the world now. I'm sure there are American outlets that need correspondents. We'll each have our own work lives and also our shared life together. It'll be wonderful."

"John—"

"But before that, we could take a vacation. Somewhere warm. Italy, Spain, Greece—you pick. Let's take a week or two and just relax."

She pulled her hand away and rubbed her eyes. "And tell me, when we return from vacation, how would you get back into the country?"

"What do you mean?"

"Your passport. You overstayed your visa by several months."

"I'll pay the fine at the airport."

"You can pay the fine for overstaying when you *leave*. But you can't pay a fine to come back in. How are you planning on getting back into the country?"

"I'll bribe the guard."

"And if that doesn't work?"

"I'll bribe his boss."

"You haven't thought this through."

"I haven't hammered out all the details. But I have thought about the important parts. I've thought about them a lot. I know that I love you. I know that I want to be with you. I know that we can make it work. Everything else is just details. Wherever you want to be is where I—"

"I love someone else."

I stopped. Took a breath. Straightened my back. Ran my finger around the rim of the wineglass.

The image of Anatoly flashed before me. Not the dream Anatoly but the real one. I felt his blood, the warmth of his blood, on my hand again. I clenched my teeth and tried to make it disappear.

"What do you mean?"

She got up and looked out the window into the courtyard. I looked to where she was looking. It was dark, but the moon and the streetlights lit the tall trees in the courtyard. The leaves were returning; you could barely see the crows' nests that had crowded the bare branches in winter.

"I'm sorry," she said. "I didn't mean for it to happen."

"Who?"

"What?"

"Who do you love?"

"I love you, John."

"But who else do you love?"

"Please."

"I just want to know."

"Does it matter?"

"Of course it matters."

She sighed. "Dima."

I got up and poured more wine. It was shattering—to finally have found her and then lost her. Not to Anatoly. Not even to what I did. To Dima. To a friend.

I took a long drink of wine. My dad had once told me that you shouldn't measure your feelings on a spectrum of happy to sad. It should be deep to shallow. Deep feelings were worthwhile, even when they were difficult. I missed him deeply. What would he say if he'd known what I'd done?

"I need to tell you something," I said. "I did something bad."

"No, please don't say that," Natalia said.

"But I did."

"Please, John, you didn't do anything bad. You cannot take responsibility for this. I am the one who did something bad."

"I'm not talking about us. You don't understand. I have to tell you something. . . ."

She pulled me into her. "Shh. No, no, no. It's okay. It's okay."

I tried not to cry, since crying in her arms now would have felt lonelier than crying alone.

"You must understand that not everything is due to you," she said softly. "You must stop apologizing for everything. I am so grateful that you came here." She stroked my hair. "This was all just a thing that happened. Leave it here and it will be wonderful to go home."

I pulled away. Held her at arm's length and looked at her. Suddenly I wasn't thinking about Anatoly anymore. "This isn't just a thing that happened. You're not just a thing that happened. We're not just a thing that happened. This matters to me."

"It matters to me, too. But sometimes it's just easier to say that it's just a thing that happened." She hugged me again.

I wanted to stay in her arms like that forever, but I knew I couldn't. I tried to just focus on that moment.

We were quiet for a long time after that. Finally, I told her I would book the next flight out. I asked if she would stay with me until then.

She looked hurt. "Of course I will stay with you. I will come with you to the airport."

I didn't think I'd be able to sleep at all that night, but we'd barely gotten under the covers before I was out. When the mattress started shaking, I thought I was in another nightmare. But then I opened my eyes and saw the morning light coming in through the window and Natalia trembling next to me. She was trying to cry quietly. I was about to reach for her when I was stopped by the realization that I hadn't dreamt of Anatoly. Not even once—not even for a second. It was like a fever had broken. I felt ready to jump out of bed with joy and wanted nothing more than to share the excitement with Natalia—but then I remembered that we were breaking up. Even if we'd stayed together, this would never be something we could share. I pulled her close to me, kissed her shoulder, held her while she cried, cried a little, too, and missed her, though she was right there next to me.

SEPTEMBER 2019

THE HEAT ON THE BUS WAS OPPRESSIVE. BUT WHEN NATALIA tried to open the window, the old lady in front of her slammed it shut. She should've known better than to try—never a bus ride without grannies who thought a light breeze would bring with it pneumonia. Most days, she did know better. But today her mind was all confused by what had happened on the tour bus the day before. On the road from Prypyat back to Kyiv, as the low evening sun heated the cabin to a boil, she had cracked open her window just a few centimeters, hoping no one would complain. A fat American woman behind her had called out, "Oh, thank you!" as if she'd performed a miracle. There were murmurs of agreement from the other passengers. So Natalia moved through the bus, all ten rows, undoing the locks and yanking open the windows to the cries of grateful Americans. All her life she'd wanted to open windows. Now rich foreigners were thanking her for doing so.

The Americans, as Oksana predicted, had poured into Ukraine to see Chernobyl. Before the TV series, Oksana would do two tours a month with groups so small she could often drive them out in her car instead of renting a bus. But since the series aired and they began their partnership, Natalia and Oksana were doing two tours per week, with fifteen to twenty-five people per tour. Oksana would take the Sunday tour, and Natalia would take the Wednesday tour, which was how she found herself spending two nights in Kyiv every week. The bus ride to Kyiv from Lutsk was brutal—six hours in the heat, bouncing over bad roads—but she often enjoyed it anyway. On the way to Kyiv, she'd be excited about all the strangers waiting in the capital to listen to her; on the ride home, she'd be pleasantly exhausted. And they were making so much money. Even accounting for operating expenses, by the end of the season Natalia would have saved over 300,000 hryvnias. More than enough to start her own tour company in Lviv.

Oksana had also correctly predicted that the tourists would like Natalia.

"You're funny," Oksana had said over their first dinner in Kyiv, the night before Natalia was to observe Oksana's tour and see if it was something she wanted to do. "And young and beautiful. The Americans will like you." She said that the Americans loved being teased and joked with. She astutely pointed out that she herself was not good with jokes; her strong suit was facts. "But, honestly, I don't think their attention spans are long enough to take in any real information."

During Oksana's tour the next day, Natalia had noticed that the Americans did begin to zone out after a while. But she wasn't sure it was because of their short attention spans. Perhaps a bigger contributing factor was that Oksana talked at them for literally ten hours, with nothing but a thirty-minute break for lunch in between. After the tour, she kept talking to Natalia through dinner, through dessert, through the walk back to the hotel, and then back in their shared room, with the lights off, until Natalia feigned sleep so theatrically that Oksana must have known she was faking. The woman never got tired. But Natalia did. And the Americans *really* did. During the short bus ride back from Prypyat to Kyiv, when Oksana was giving a lecture on the history of Ukrainian freeways, the Americans' eyes were desperate, pleading. *Please. Just a little silence.*

Natalia had decided right then that she would employ the American style for her tours—be lighter, mix in jokes. She soon found that this Americanization came, if not naturally, at least easily. She suspected that she would have been more nervous, telling jokes in a second language being as intimidating as it was, if not for her time answering phones—but also her time with John. He liked it when she was funny. He liked being teased. She couldn't imagine talking to strangers the way she talked to him, but it still helped. Since he'd left, sometimes she'd wake up in the morning and miss the feel of his body. When she walked around the park alone, she missed the feel of their early walks, the electricity of possibility, his barely restrained desire for her. It still made her sad to remember the sight of him walking away at the airport, both of them trying to hold back tears. But, at the same time, she didn't miss him at all. It was hard to explain, feeling two contradictory things so strongly at once.

The bus driver pulled into the rest stop they always stopped at, about halfway between Kyiv and Lutsk.

He turned off the engine and said, "Fifteen minutes."

Everyone got out. It was hot and the rest stop didn't smell good, but still—the feel of air after the stuffy bus was something. Natalia headed to the toilets. She still carried toilet paper around in her purse as a matter of habit, even though a decreasing number of places had squat toilets anymore and most of the modern toilets were now stocked with toilet paper. Once, while she was giving a tour to the Americans, reaching for her phone to check the time, her toilet paper had fallen out of her purse. She had been briefly horrified before regaining herself.

"My mother used to say that you must always be prepared," she had told the tour, though her mother had never said that.

"Like the Boy Scouts!" a middle-aged man had called out.

"Do you have Boy Scouts here?" a woman asked.

"We used to," Natalia said. "They were called the Red Army. Like the Boy Scouts, but with less cookies."

Oksana would have told them about the Pioneers—would have talked them to sleep about the Pioneers—but Natalia knew the difference between a real question and an invitation to banter. She had quickly learned what little bits of knowledge Americans had about Ukraine and the Soviet Union, and what they would find funny based on this limited knowledge. She saved the informative stuff for the topic they paid for: Chernobyl. Otherwise, she went with the jokes. And did the Americans love the jokes! They howled, slapped their knees, and repeated the punch lines.

"Less cookies!" the middle-aged man had repeated to his wife. He wore a baseball cap with an *M* on it, a T-shirt that said *Six Flags* tucked into denim shorts, and white sneakers with white socks. She had been surprised to learn that most American men dressed just as badly as Ukrainian men—but in a totally different way. Ukrainian men dressed like lazy boys. American men dressed like they had chosen their outfits from a box of donations following a disaster.

"Maybe they've been disabled by too much choice," she'd theorized to Oksana over lattes one afternoon. "If you can choose between every brand of clothing in the world, maybe you get color-blind."

"No, no, no. It's just power. Why dress up when you don't have to?" Oksana had said, her carefully manicured red nails tightly wrapped around the cup like it might try to escape.

Natalia paid the woman behind the window the two hryvnias to use the toilet. But when she got inside and saw the squat toilet, she found that she didn't have to go. She took a breath, fixed her hair in the mirror, and ran the water over her hands. The woman taking the money hadn't said anything when Natalia paid her. Why would she?

But John always commented on the "amazingly" wordless nature of these interactions, and now Natalia couldn't help but notice. What were you supposed to say to someone who pays you money to use the toilet? *Have a good wee*?

John would have laughed. She pulled out her phone to check his social media, as she still did from time to time—though not nearly as frequently as she had in the weeks after his departure. She didn't do it anxiously anymore—more like you'd check the news when you found your fingers idle. Since he'd left, he'd only posted three times. One was a video of a park with a large garden of roses and a fountain in the background, with John, two other boys, and two girls, smiling into the camera. John wore a white T-shirt with the sleeves slightly rolled up and a new pair of jeans. He looked tanner. *Back in Portland!* the caption read. The four other people in the photo—she'd been relieved to learn after searching across accounts months ago—were coupled together.

The second post was of a sign that said: *Portland Community College*. The caption read: *Excited to be earning my certificate in Teaching English as a Second Language. Hopefully in the process I will finally learn to speak English as a first language.*

The last post was of John in a navy-blue suit jacket with no tie and the top button of his shirt unbuttoned, standing with his arm around a short, fat man who was dressed in a tie with his shirtsleeves rolled up, both of them smiling warmly. Behind them was a gold plaque: *Richard Turner 1950–2017*. The caption read: *I am very grateful to @Gene.58.Law for this wonderful tribute to my dad, who was loved by everyone who knew him. Except for the plaintiffs.*

He'd never mentioned his father, even when she talked about hers. She hadn't found it odd then. But she did after seeing the picture. That night when she'd talked about her father and the end of her ballet career, John had just said, "I understand." Was it because he didn't want her to know him that well when he'd be leaving her soon? No, that didn't make sense. She'd been the one who'd broken up with him. Why would he be holding back when he so clearly wanted her—when he had wanted her so badly that he had leaned over and kissed her in his kitchen as soon as she came back from her sister's, right as she was talking about her dead husband? That was not the behavior of a man holding back. With every passing day, the past made less sense.

Outside, half the passengers were smoking. The old ladies sat on the bench eating sandwiches they'd unwrapped from their plastic shopping bags. Natalia stood in the shade of the overhang and watched a woman offer some bread to a stray dog. The dog sniffed it and walked away.

"Spoiled!" the woman exclaimed to no one in particular.

The driver returned with a paper cup of coffee, and they reboarded the hot bus. Natalia looked out at the big empty fields passing through the window, dotted with occasional clusters of houses. It hadn't even been twenty-four hours since the tour ended, but she already longed for another audience. The season would soon be over. Even if her new business went well, it would take a while to build up a customer base in Lviv. At best, she would be giving regular tours the following summer. She missed the Americans already.

The bus finally reached its Lutsk stop, near the Tam Tam shopping center, at six in the evening. She hadn't enjoyed the trip home the way she usually did. She was hot, irritated, and feeling pessimistic about the future. Nothing had really changed since the ride to Kyiv, two days earlier, when she'd felt optimistic about the future. But that was life—things just changed for no reason. She wasn't looking forward to a suffocating ride back to her apartment on the city bus, stopping every other block while the grannies gripped the windows closed with their knobby hands. She decided to splurge on a taxi. After all, she could afford it.

She walked over to a blue Volkswagen from the nineties with a Joker Taxi lamp on the roof. The driver was reading a book. He looked up when she opened the door and started the car when she gave him the address. She rolled down the window and closed her eyes to feel the air against her face.

"Close the window!" the driver barked. "I have papers in here."

She didn't feel like arguing. But she was annoyed. She was spending sixty hryvnias to have a comfortable ride. And now she couldn't even do that.

She had been considering taking a vacation after tour season ended. Some place with beaches and bright white houses. She wanted to walk around in a postcard for a while, see how it felt. Lie out on a beach chair, a glass of rosé in hand, no one to talk to and nothing to do. But how long would a vacation alone be nice for? When she came home from the tours in Kyiv, she still loved the feeling of walking into her apartment without having to brace for someone else's reaction. The way she didn't have to wonder what mood someone else would be in and how that mood would dictate the shape of her day. The way she could watch Korean soap operas without anyone judging her. The way she could just feel whatever she wanted to feel without preparation or planning. But after a day or so back from the capital, she'd get a little bored. A little sad, even. By Tuesday morning she'd be itching for the bus back to Kyiv. There weren't enough walks in the day, enough tea with friends, enough visiting her sister, to fill all that time. She fiddled with the ring on her right-hand ring finger.

"My husband wouldn't appreciate it," she would say when the Americans asked her out, and point to her ring. If she wanted to stop them, she could have switched it over to the left hand—the American side. But that would have been too much.

The men would apologize and say something like, "He's a lucky man."

It was much easier for them to accept that she was the property of another man than that she wasn't interested in them. It was the same with John. She still couldn't believe that he'd so easily swallowed her lie about Dima. She'd just blurted it out from frustration! She'd just as soon date a cousin. But John had believed her. All her protestations about why it didn't make sense for them to stay together, about how he was asking her to wager her future on the constancy of his feelings, were nothing compared to the idea of her belonging to Dima. Maybe it was her fault for not being able to communicate to him what it was about his proposition that was so impossible. But she suspected that, even if she had been better at English, or if he had spoken Ukrainian, he still wouldn't have understood.

The driver stopped in front of her building. She handed him a fifty and a twenty and waited for change on the sixty-four-hryvnia fare. John would have been appalled to see her cheap out on a six-hryvnia tip. *That's twenty-five cents!* he would say, as if translating it into American currency would make it more real. But why should she reward the driver for his poor service? What was the point of a merit-based reward if it was not based on merit?

She hated the walk up the stairs to her apartment. It still nauseated her, even so many months later. It had been easier when she'd been taking the stairs to John's apartment, but John's apartment was once again occupied by Bohdan, who'd found that Airbnb wasn't worth it when there was no American renting by the month. It had been nice having John next door, even in the beginning, before he knew they were neighbors, because he never thought it was her fault. Not that she needed to be reassured. Deep down, she knew it wasn't her fault.

It was Anatoly's. But her mind kept feeding her lies. Maybe there wouldn't be problems if she didn't pick at Anatoly. It must be hard for him that things hadn't worked out the way he'd hoped. Things were going so well for her—why couldn't she just support him? But then one night someone pounded on the door, and Anatoly stopped, and she stopped, and all those thoughts stopped, just for a moment, and for that moment she saw it clearly for what it was.

Of course, when the moment ended she was exactly the same and Anatoly was exactly the same, and the exact same life was waiting for her on the other side. But still. It was nice to have that moment, since she couldn't really talk to anyone about it. Her sister would have said, *But what did you say? Why did you upset him? You know how you are.* Why should she complain about Anatoly? Anatoly was a dream! He corrected Oleksander when he drank too much and started talking stupid. He leaned down to eye level to talk to children. Her mother was too self-centered and, frankly speaking, a little too dumb to be of any help. She viewed other people's problems as inconveniences that kept her from talking about herself. And Anatoly was so handsome! What a gentleman. She could have talked to her father, maybe, if he was still alive. But it would have upset him so much that she probably would have hidden it from him, too.

Katinka and Yuliya were of no use either. Anatoly was so much more charming, thoughtful, and handsome than their husbands. He complimented them on their haircuts! They loved Anatoly, which was funny, since according to Anatoly, they were the ones who'd turned his wife against him. He believed that their marital problems had started when she and the girls had gone to Amsterdam. The trip had, admittedly, been a little more expensive than she had planned. Anatoly was right about that part, and he had been making more money than her at the time. And yes, it was a little embarrassing to stay in a youth hostel with two other married women when they were all thirty. But it hadn't turned her against Anatoly at all. If anything, it made her a happier, fuller person, capable of a happier, fuller life. Suddenly, after Maidan, there was no astronomical visa fee to visit Europe—just a guard welcoming you at the border. *Please, come in, stay for ninety days if you like.* Her passport, so long a key without a lock, now opened a whole continent. And they were barely at the hostel anyway. They were busy exploring the most incredible place she'd ever seen.

Amsterdam wasn't incredible because of the bridges, the bicycles, and the gingerbread houses reflecting off the canals—those were all nice, sure, but there were parts of Kyiv or Lviv that were just as beautiful. What was incredible was that the city *functioned.* When there was no one at the top skimming all the best jobs, apartments, appointments, and contracts, this was what could happen. This was what happened when you hired the most qualified people instead of the best-connected people. Buses and trains ran on time, buildings were clean, everyone was healthy, there were wonderful places to eat and drink, and even at rush hour, when the people bustled shoulder to shoulder and the cars wedged bumper to bumper, the city was calm.

One of the first thoughts she'd had upon arriving was that she wanted to show it to Anatoly. He could have been a different person if they'd grown up in a place like this. A place where journalists weren't beaten because they'd written about government contracts going to a factory that produced nothing. She understood why he'd given up after that. They'd broken his arm, cracked his ribs. He'd had headaches for months after. And being attacked by surprise made you expect an attack all the time. He'd been ashamed. It was a terrible way to live. Giving up had been the smart thing to do. He wasn't going to change anything with his articles, and they could very well get him killed. But in her less generous moments, she thought that maybe he'd been looking for a reason to give up. That when he got out into the world and found that his talent wasn't quite as great as he imagined, his ideas not quite as original as he'd thought, and his genius not actually genius but just intelligence, he'd never fully recovered from the blow. If he'd been in a place like Amsterdam, maybe he would have had the chance to recover. That was the biggest difference between a Ukrainian and a European. Or an American. The world offered maybe one chance to a Ukrainian. Europeans and Americans could keep coming back as many times as they wished.

On their last night in Amsterdam, after full days of walking the free gardens, visiting the cheapest museums, and eating hamburgers and kebabs, she and the girls had decided to splurge on a fashionable wine bar they passed every night on their way back to the hostel. At first, Natalia had felt out of place in that dimly lit room full of hip, wealthy Dutch people. But soon she realized that the looks she was attracting were not because she was dressed wrong but because she was more beautiful than the Dutch women. When a man approached the table and asked if he could buy them a bottle of wine, instead of waving him off, Natalia said, "If you like, but we will not be talking with you."

"As long as you're drinking with me," the man said, and laughed.

He was tall, slim, and Nordic looking, with a shaved head that boasted a suntan despite it being March. His short blond beard looked like it had been lined up with a very sharp blade. His suit was skinny and expensive, a shade of olive that Natalia didn't see often, even on rich businessmen. He sat down and asked where they were visiting from.

"We're visiting from Ukraine," Yuliya said, in triumphant English.

He answered that he'd once been to Ukraine on business. It was a beautiful place, he thought, so full of beauty.

"You must not have ridden the buses," said Natalia.

"No, I was only there for a short stay and I didn't immerse myself in the culture as fully as I should have."

What a funny affectation—to apologize for not doing things you had enough money to avoid. If Natalia could afford it, she would never take the bus.

The wine arrived, and the Nordic-looking man poured it out evenly between their four glasses, holding the bottle by the bottom.

"When I was in Kyiv," he said, "it was winter and the whole city was covered in ice. I could barely keep my balance. But the women—they were walking around in high heels like it was nothing! How is it," he said, turning to look at Natalia, "that you can walk across ice in high heels without falling?"

"The secret," Natalia said, taking a sip of wine to draw out the suspense, then lowering her voice ever so slightly, "is that we fall all the time."

The man laughed in appreciation. But there was something performative about the laugh. He seemed to be wanting admiration for laughing at her joke, while also waiting for admiration about his own observation—for Natalia to react to his ability to notice that a woman's attire might affect her mobility.

"If the shoes make you fall all the time," the man said, once it became clear that no compliment was coming, "why do you wear them?"

"The same reason boxers take steroids," Natalia said. She was getting a little light-headed from the wine and was maybe saying too much. One of the other girls should say something so the man didn't think they were alone. Natalia wasn't going to sleep with him and she didn't want him to think that she was. But they didn't say anything, so Natalia continued: "We wear them to compete."

But she wasn't in Amsterdam to hear this Dutch guy talk about

Ukraine. She wanted to hear about Amsterdam. She wanted to learn how someone went about getting a job in a place like this.

"Do you own a business here?" she said.

"In Amsterdam?" the man said. "No, I work for a consulting firm in Copenhagen."

"But you are from here?"

"From Holland?" He laughed. "No, I'm from Denmark."

"How long have you been in Amsterdam?"

"This is my first night, actually," the man said. "Have you seen anything that you'd recommend?"

At least he paid for the wine and didn't pout when the girls left without him. He wished them good night, complimented her shoes, and warned her to be careful walking home in those heels.

It had been a point of contention that she'd packed the shoes for her trip, since, by that point in their marriage, Natalia rarely wore high heels. This bothered Anatoly, who felt that it reflected poorly on him. But he was a man easily bothered. A headache could cripple him. A canceled bus could ruin his day. The funny thing was that, when it came to real problems, he was strong and stable—decisive but kind. Like after her father died and Anatoly had made all the difficult decisions and arrangements so that she could mourn. Later, after Anatoly died, she kept longing for Anatoly to help her cope with his death. When he hit her hard, it was in the stomach. Sometimes on the arm but not hard enough to break it. Sometimes he slapped her on the side of the head. But until the end, he rarely hit anywhere that would leave a bruise visible to others. When she saw he was going to strike, it was terrifying. She feared the pain; it was worse knowing how much it would hurt. But it was almost like when the nausea rises into vomit and you know that after the terribleness, relief is coming. He never hit her more than once at a time. And he was never a better husband than the day after he hit her.

When she reached the top of the stairs and got inside, her apartment was stuffy and warm, just like the bus. Just like the taxi with the idiot driver. She marched straight to the kitchen without even taking off her shoes and opened the window. The evening air spilled in like water. She felt her whole body relax. She just stood there for a moment, not bracing for anything.

Anatoly would let the window be open sometimes but only when he opened it. If she tried to change the temperature in any way, he would complain that at a different point in time she had wanted a different temperature. *Now you're hot, but tonight you'll need an extra blanket!* It proved her inconstancy and unreliability. Of course, when his temperature changed, it was because he was hot from working. Strange that she still found herself having these arguments with him, even now that he'd been dead for eight months. She wondered if they would ever stop.

When she'd found him lying there that night, for a terrible second, she'd thought he was dead. She screamed, ran to him, fell to her knees, and called out his name again and again.

But he wasn't dead.

He opened his eyes—labored them open like he was waking up with a hangover. He'd whispered, "It hurts." Then he'd blinked a few times slowly, like he was going to go back to sleep, but kept his eyes open.

It hurts.

For him, it hurt.

Of course it hurt. That was life. It hurt when he hit her. It hurt that he was making her abandon her life in Lutsk. It hurt to know that she could never fully escape him.

A few days before that, over the New Year's holiday, she'd been out for lunch with Oksana. Anatoly's mood had been getting worse lately, more unpredictable. And while Natalia didn't normally discuss such personal things with Oksana, there was something about her that day that felt particularly open and inviting. So Natalia did something she had never done before: she told Oksana about her marriage.

Oksana listened to her as she laid it all out in a breathless cascade.

"What are you going to do?" Oksana finally said.

"What do you mean?"

"I mean, will you stay or will you leave?"

"I don't have much of a choice," Natalia said.

"No, not much of a choice," Oksana agreed. "But in your case, there is a choice."

They were quiet for a while.

Oksana said, "It's important to know the difference between the things that you're willing to tolerate and the things that you aren't. The things you're willing to tolerate can be bad, so long as the alternative is worse. Decide for yourself what you're willing to tolerate. And if his actions surpass your tolerance, you must leave."

"What are you willing to tolerate?" Natalia said.

Oksana called over the waitress and told her to bring them each another latte. Natalia had never seen Oksana order a second coffee before.

"I once read an article about husbands who hit their wives," Oksana said. "The husbands who punch and slap their wives almost never kill them. Okay, it's not good. Yet it's often tolerable. But then there are the husbands who choke their wives. Men who have choked their wives at least once are far more likely to murder them than men who just hit their wives. Choking is a sign that they are willing to kill. So for me, that is the line. I'm not willing to tolerate the possibility that my husband might kill me. Viktor has never choked me. But if he ever did, I would leave the very next day."

The day after Anatoly choked her, Natalia was in a daze. She was out of her mind with anger and guilt, disoriented from the dialogue she'd been having with herself all night. She was ashamed and confused and so full of rage that she felt she couldn't speak. But then John was standing in front of her, and when she saw John's reaction to her bruises, his shock and worry and panic, all her emotions sharpened into focus. She went straight to Oksana's, and when Oksana opened the door Natalia removed her scarf. Oksana didn't ask any questions, just brought her inside and started planning Natalia's departure. Natalia would go to bed that night like it was any other night so that Anatoly wouldn't suspect anything. But once he fell asleep, she would call Oksana, who would pick her up and drive her through the anonymous night to Kyiv. Anatoly always slept like a corpse after a shift; she'd be in the capital before he woke. Oksana's son was home for the holidays, so Natalia would stay in his apartment in Kyiv while she decided on her next move.

But when Natalia came home that evening, ready to pretend that everything was okay one last time, there he was on the floor. Bleeding. Begging. Insisting on her sympathy and care. *It hurts.* As if she were the one who'd hit him! As if she were the one who'd done this. The pillow was in her hands before she even thought about it. It wasn't a choice—it just happened. He barely struggled at first, then more, with his arms flailing and punching. But that night, he was weak, and before long, it was over.

After, she sat frozen. She called his name and tried to wake him up. She shook him and tried to wake him. But he was gone. She'd cried. Of course she'd cried—she wasn't a monster. She'd missed him immediately.

Now she sat down at the dinner table, poured herself a glass of wine, and missed him again. Her muscles were sore from all the bus sitting. She felt terrible about what she'd done. But as much as she tried, she couldn't regret it. Or, if she did, it wasn't true regret. She didn't regret that he was dead—only that she was the one who'd done it. She regretted that the memory would be forever stored in her brain and would probably prevent her from ever fully loving again.

She didn't believe in an afterlife. She didn't disbelieve in it either, but it didn't seem prudent to plan for a windfall you had no evidence was coming—better to be pleasantly surprised in the event that it arrived. She went off the assumption that when you died you went from living to nothing. Which meant that dying was only tragic if the nothing of death was worse than the something of life. If Anatoly had died when he was twenty-four, when Natalia met him, it would have been tragic. His life was so full and happy. It would have probably been tragic even at thirty-four. But he was thirty-eight when he died, and his existence was already running out of things to offer him. He'd enjoyed his early life. Why wouldn't he? He'd been a golden child. But lately, the things that brought him joy—that he was handsome, charming, clever, and well-liked—were fading. His hair had started to go and his belly had begun to grow. His jokes were duller, his mind not as quick, his understanding of current events more tenuous, and his general demeanor angrier and more bitter. He was decaying. So was she, of course. But her world was expanding while his was contracting.

They'd lived most of their lives as slaves. Now a revolution had come—or the closest thing to revolution that you got in real life. And she was ready for it. But Anatoly was too scared. He'd have aged into one of those uncles who'd seen the Soviet Union collapse just as they'd passed the age where they could be filled with excitement instead of fear. The men who longed for the good old days when everyone was equal in suffering. The world was no longer for these uncles. Nor was it for Anatoly. Hers had been an act of mercy.

She was suspicious of this line of thinking, of course, as it reeked of rationalization. How could she know how Anatoly would have turned out? He could have changed. Maybe he would have turned forty and started a new chapter. Maybe they would have decided to have a child and fatherhood would have made a better man out of him. Maybe the rest of his life would've been good or maybe it would've been bad. She couldn't know. But she knew this much: Anatoly had been suffering and now he wasn't.

In the days that followed his death, she had been full of grief—brimming over with it. She cried over pictures of him, memories of his jokes, his touch, and the way he held her. She missed her idea of what he could be, the one she'd clung to while he was alive—the man he'd been in the past and might be again. She missed having that door of possibility open—not fully open, but not slammed shut either, like it was now. When she'd grieved for her father, she would have given anything for another day with him—just to sit with him and get to hear him laugh again. With Anatoly's death, she'd learned that it was possible to miss someone and also be glad that they weren't coming back.

But what was the point of all this? What was the point of going over the same thoughts over and over? She finished the wine and set down the glass. The past was gone. She had to stop. She stood up and looked out the open window. Soon the air would turn cold and the leaves would fall again, but today the branches were thick with green—oblivious to the change that was coming. She wanted to think of something else. With the taste of wine on her tongue and the breeze in her face, she tried to find something to rest her eyes on. Trees, clotheslines, sky. She settled on her reflection. Her hair was fluttering slightly. Her eyebrows needed some tending after the long trip home. But she liked the reflection. As she watched it, she kept thinking of a scene from a thriller, one she'd seen in the theaters years ago, when a girl is looking in her mirror and then, all of a sudden, a terrifying second face appears behind her. She kept bracing for another reflection to flash behind hers. She kept waiting for it to suddenly appear, demanding her attention, demanding her fear. But there was no one else home. She could do whatever she wanted.

ACKNOWLEDGMENTS

Thank you to all my friends in Ukraine, especially Ramiz Abbasov, Lev Boyko, and Nazar Romanchenko. I am indebted to them for helping me understand Ukraine but even more so for making Lutsk feel like home. Special thanks to Lev, who, when my coworking space unexpectedly closed, found me an empty desk at a customer support office so that I would have somewhere to write.

Thank you to Ella Yatsuta, of the Frontera Festival and the ANGAR charitable organization in Lutsk, for helping me understand the important role of Ukrainian art in shaping the modern Ukrainian consciousness, and to the volunteers at ANGAR, for their tireless efforts to liberate Ukraine from Russian tyranny.

Thank you to my Ukrainian fact-checking editor, Olena Kotys, associate professor of Lesya Ukrainka Volyn National University in Lutsk, for providing astute and valuable insight during such a difficult time. For expertise in GBV response in Ukraine, thank you to Camilla Marthinsen. For expertise in customer support ops, thank you to Jake Howell. None of the abovementioned is responsible for any mistakes of fact that may have slipped into the book, but they are responsible for correcting the ones that didn't.

Thank you to my agent, Chris Clemans—simply the best, in every way. To my editor, Marysue Rucci, who bought this book based on just five pages—an act of faith that allowed me to write the rest. To the fantastic Zack Knoll and Brittany Adames, for their early work on the book, and to Andy Tang, for bringing us across the finish line.

Thank you to my first readers: Peter Baker, Sherilyn Harrington, and Robert Siegel.

Thank you to my family, for constant love and encouragement.

Finally, thank you to Sherilyn, who brought me to Ukraine. Every day, out of all the ways she could spend that day, she chooses to spend it loving me. What luck.

ABOUT THE AUTHOR

Johannes Lichtman's first novel, *Such Good Work*, was chosen as a 5 Under 35 honoree by the National Book Foundation. He lives in Washington, DC.